THE NANNY AND THE ALIEN WARRIOR

TREASURED BY THE ALIEN

HONEY PHILLIPS

BEX MCLYNN

CHAPTER ONE

"This way. Hurry," Sultavi urged.

Joanna clutched her cloak closer to her neck with one hand and tightened her grip on the little girl with the other.

"Are you sure?" she whispered as Sultavi led them down a back alley in the warren of buildings that made up the commercial center of Isokau, the main city in Lord K'herr's domain.

The market wasn't asleep—it never truly slept—but at this hour, most of the activity was concentrated around the bars and the gambling houses. The shops surrounding them were dark and still.

"I'm sure." Sultavi spoke with the absolute confidence of a precocious six-year-old, but Joanna wasn't convinced.

They had been to the market many times before, but they had always been accompanied by Lord K'herr's guards. She was no fan of the big warriors—they were there to prevent her from escaping as much as to protect Sultavi—but right now she would have welcomed a few bodies surrounding them as they hurried down the dark passageway.

But they were all dead, and she and Sultavi were on their own.

A lump formed in her throat. Even though she hadn't cared for the guards, they had never treated her badly. *With one exception,* she thought with a shudder. And now they were all gone.

Nohta, the captain of the guards, had been the one to rouse her a short time ago, thrusting a confused Sultavi into her arms.

"Take the girl. We have to go."

She hadn't argued, pausing only long enough to throw a cloak over her nightclothes before lifting the girl into her arms. Sultavi had already been wrapped in a dark uniform shirt, her face pale and scared.

"What's wrong?" she whispered as Nohta set off at a rapid pace through the extensive gardens that were part of the House Sodan compound. She could hear the sounds of fighting in the distance and see flames burning at the rear of the main building.

"Father is dead," Sultavi said, a tear rolling down her cheek. Her body quivered in Joanna's arms, but she seemed to understand the need for silence.

"We were betrayed," Nohta said grimly.

Her mind flew back to the previous evening. Sultavi had been dressed in her finest clothes and taken off to some type of ceremonial banquet for a visiting relative—a cousin of some kind. Joanna had been forbidden to accompany her, but she'd been waiting when the little girl returned, tired and grumpy. The ceremonial outfit was uncomfortable, the food had been "yucky," and she didn't like her father's visitor.

"Who was he?" she asked as she unfastened the ceremonial braids and brushed out Sultavi's long purple hair.

"Lord T'paja." The little girl yawned. "A third cousin once

removed on my father's side. His father was Lord T'norwa, who lost his estate in a card game."

Joanna wasn't surprised that Sultavi knew all the details of the family lineage. Lord K'herr was raising his daughter as the future leader of their House.

"There. All finished." She smoothed down the last shining strand and dropped a kiss on the little girl's head, then helped her up into the big bed. "Why didn't you like him?"

"He talked to me like I was stupid." A frown made the tiny dark horns pull together. "He said if I came to visit him, he'd give me a dolly. I'm not a baby."

"If you went to visit him?"

Joanna's heart skipped a beat. As much as she hated being a prisoner, she knew what to expect in Lord K'herr's compound. Another Allikan lord might not afford her the same protection. But it was almost worse to think of Sultavi going without her. She loved the little girl like her own child.

"Father didn't like that idea. He made one of his mean faces." Sultavi giggled. "So then I *accidentally* spilled my juice on Lord T'paja's robes."

"Tavi, you shouldn't have done that. You know your father expects you to be on your best behavior."

The girl shrugged. "I don't think he minded. He told me it was time for bed, but his eyes were smiling. I wish they did that more often."

"I know, sweetheart," Joanna said sympathetically.

She honestly believed that Lord K'herr loved his daughter, but he didn't seem to know how to express it. It didn't help that he always seemed to be busy. Other than meeting with Sultavi once a week to instruct her on her future duties, he rarely saw the child.

"It's late. You should go to sleep."

"I want a story. Please." Big purple eyes gave her a pleading look, and Joanna succumbed.

"All right. But just a short one. Once upon a time..."

Sultavi's usual determination to stay awake long enough to hear the end of the story was defeated by exhaustion from the late night. Her eyes were closed before Joanna had even reached the midpoint of her tale. Joanna kissed her again, tucked the covers around her, and went off to her own bed in the small adjoining room.

Who would have thought that she would have ended up using her doctorate in medieval history to come up with stories to tell the daughter of an alien warlord, she thought as she prepared for bed. Her usual day outfit was a simple gown in the colors of House Sodan—with the insignia that marked her as its property—but the House tailor had made her a white tunic and pants for sleeping.

Before she climbed into bed, she added the day's notch to the collection of scratches she used to track her time in captivity, then froze as she took in the neat squares.

A year. She had been on this alien world for a year now.

A lump caught in her throat. There were times when life on Earth seemed like nothing more than a distant dream, or times like now when she still couldn't believe what had happened to her.

She had been walking home after an evening class. The campus was quiet, the shadows heavy between the lamp posts, but it hadn't occurred to her to be afraid. And then she'd heard a muffled cry from under the trees lining the path. Even then, she'd simply thought that someone might have hurt themselves and had gone to help.

Only to discover a white-skinned man bending down over the limp body of a female student. She'd opened her mouth to call for help, and then a blinding pain shot through her shoulder and the world went dark.

When she awoke, she was in a small white cell barely large enough for a metal cot. A glass wall at one end of the cell revealed two of the white-skinned men standing there, staring at her.

Not men, she realized with a sickening thud as she took in the details she had missed in the dark night. White, almost plastic-like skin, matte black hair like that of an animal, and eyes that held an eerie red glow.

She was still staring at them when she realized that she could understand what they were saying, even though she was quite sure they weren't speaking English.

"I don't know. I think she's too old," the first one said.

Too old for what?

"For breeding maybe." The second speaker shrugged. "But the captain says there's a demand for all types of females."

"He'd better be right. I have plans for my share of the profits."

"We couldn't leave her alive after she saw us." Another shrug. "And a meager profit is better than none."

Breeding? Profit? Her mind still struggled to make sense of the situation, but she pulled herself to her feet and went to the glass wall.

"Let me out of here. You can't do this," she protested, but even as she spoke she knew it was a stupid thing to say.

The first male seemed to agree, smirking at her. "We can and we have."

He scanned her up and down, his eyes cold and assessing. "I just hope some of our customers prefer a more... seasoned product."

Before she could respond, his companion tapped him on the arm. "Come. Let's go evaluate the rest of the stock."

They disappeared down the white corridor, and she sank back down on her bunk.

Aliens. She had been kidnapped by aliens.

Her rational mind wanted to scream a protest, but it all seemed a little too real—from the faint medicinal tang in the air to the smug certainty on the face of her captors. She examined her cell thoroughly, looking for a way out, but she couldn't even find anything resembling a control by the glass panel. The rear of the cell did contain a concealed panel that led into a tiny bathroom, but she found nothing else.

As she sank back down on her bunk, she thought longingly of her friend June. The other woman was a whiz with anything computer-operated and could no doubt have hacked her way out. Joanna's skills did not lie in that direction.

Her captivity settled into a monotonous routine. The lights would dim periodically, and when they brightened, an alien would come by and thrust a tray of bland food through an opening that appeared in the glass wall. She could never determine how he made it open, or figure out a way to take advantage of the situation. And as the time dripped by, they were getting further away from Earth and any chance of escape.

Nothing else broke up the monotony except nightmarish visions of the possible fate that awaited her at the end of the journey. She had no illusions about her value on a slave market, especially if they wanted breeders. Theoretically, she was still capable of bearing children, but the chances were low at her age. And while she was fine with her appearance, straight brown hair, ordinary brown eyes, and a short, plump body didn't tend to inspire lust in the male breast. *But maybe that's a good thing under the circumstances*, she thought dryly.

To keep boredom—and terror—at bay, she spent her time reviewing her latest research paper in her head, or reciting medieval poetry. She had gotten so used to the routine that when an alien appeared at the wall of her cell in the middle of the day, she was actually surprised.

The glass panel slid aside.

"Come, human. It's time for you to establish your worth."

The voice sounded familiar, and she thought she recognized him as one of the ones she had seen on her first day.

"I know my worth, thank you very much," she said, her teeth gritted.

"That is irrelevant. The only worth that matters is how many credits someone will pay for you. Now come."

He grabbed her arm—six fingers cold and surprisingly strong—and hauled her to her feet. She instinctively started to struggle and he yanked her arm up behind her back until it felt like it was on the edge of breaking.

"Do not try my patience. An unconscious female has less value, but she will still sell. Is that what you want?"

She shuddered. The idea of being unconscious while her fate was decided horrified her.

"I don't want that," she whispered.

"Then behave."

He released her aching arm, then prodded her out into the corridor. More women, most of them the age of her college students, were emerging from similar cells. Their expressions ranged from panic to shock, and many of them were crying as the white-skinned aliens prodded them along. She wanted to slow down, to speak to some of them, but her captor hurried her out in front of the others.

"We might have an offer for you. Better hope it works out," he hissed.

"Offer? What offer?"

"Just shut up and keep moving."

He pulled her along the corridor, then out of the ship and down a ramp. They were in a vast enclosed building, like a huge airplane hangar, with what looked like a makeshift stage in front of the ship. Beyond the stage, a dizzying array of aliens milled around with glasses in their hands, or claws, or tentacles. She just had time to notice that they all seemed to be dressed in elaborate clothing, with jewels sparkling in some extremely strange places, before her captor marched her down a set of steps and away from the stage.

The noise behind her increased as the other women began to emerge from the ship and saw the stage and the waiting audience. Their frantic cries mixed with appreciative sounds from waiting aliens - everything from growls to clicks to hisses. Her guard ignored the racket, leading her to a door on the outer wall of the building. He thrust her through it into a small room, blessedly quiet after the turmoil outside, and slammed the door behind her.

Only one other person occupied the room, a big alien with dark purple hair pulled back from two curved horns and plaited in a single long braid. Unlike the glimpses she'd had of the other customers, he wasn't festooned in luxurious fabrics or dripping with jewels. He wore a simple leather vest with a small insignia on his shoulder, but the lack of finery did nothing to lessen his air of command. She was quite sure he was a male used to being in charge.

But he's not in charge of me, she thought defiantly.

She straightened her shoulders, raised her chin, and did her best not to flinch under his cold, thoughtful gaze as he surveyed her.

"I have a daughter," he said finally.

It wasn't what she had expected him to say, and she frowned at him.

"She needs a female to look after her," he continued.

"What about your wife?" she asked tentatively.

His face grew even colder. "My mate is dead."

She felt an unexpected pang of sympathy, but from his expression she suspected he wouldn't welcome such a sentiment from her. *He's an alien slaveowner,* she reminded herself. *He doesn't deserve compassion.*

"Our race does not have many females." His fists clenched at his sides. "The few who exist are spoiled schemers. They would not treat Sultavi well."

"Why not? If females are rare—"

"They would see her as competition for their own child. Perhaps even as competition for my... affections."

"I'm sorry, but what's that got to do with me?"

He sighed, and for a moment she saw weariness cross the hard face. "Since the Red Death, all females are in short supply. The female companions I have hired for my daughter were all lured away by males desperate for mates. As a slave, you will not have that option."

Her stomach clenched at the complete certainty in his statement. *I am not a slave,* she thought defiantly, but despite her resistance, she couldn't see a way out of the situation.

"Why me?" she asked again.

"You are a mature female, and your sales packet states that you are educated, despite your primitive background." The skepticism was quite obvious. "Sultavi needs the care of a female. You appear to be the best option."

"But I don't belong here. I have a life back on Earth." A safe, peaceful life with her books and her classes and her plants.

"That life is over." There wasn't a trace of remorse on his face. "I'm offering you an alternative. Unless you'd prefer to be auctioned off for more... physical purposes? Your age would be against you," he added dispassionately. "But as I said, females are in demand."

She shuddered, remembering the raucous crowd outside.

"I don't want that," she said quietly.

"Then I will make the arrangements." He didn't seem to have had the slightest doubt that she would agree, exiting the room without a backwards glance.

She had still been thinking of that long ago day when Captain Nohta had found her. Now she and the little girl she loved so much were on the run and everything had changed once again.

CHAPTER TWO

"That's it," Sultavi whispered, pointing to a pink house perched on short poles and drawing Joanna's attention back to the present.

They had reached the edge of the market and the beginning of the residential district. The row of small houses that lined the street varied wildly in color and style, but they were all neat and well-kept with attractive gardens. The pink house was the exception, the jungle of plants that surrounded it looking completely out of control.

"Are you sure, Tavi?" Joanna asked again.

"Yes. My last nanny used to bring me to tea here sometimes. She was Trevelorian too."

A clatter of noise sounded from further up the street, and Joanna pulled the girl back into the shadows, her heart pounding wildly. The sounds faded but she couldn't quite force herself to leave the safety of the dark patch.

"That's the one who got mated and moved away, right?"

"Yes. I was sad. But then Father brought you to me and everything was all right again."

Sultavi gave her a sweet smile, and Joanna's chest ached. She'd never quite been able to tell the girl that she was only here because she had no choice. But was that still true? Even if someone magically offered her a way home, she didn't think she could leave Tavi.

She shook her head. Right now, staying out of Lord T'paja's clutches was more important than a theoretical choice to return to Earth.

"All right. Let's go while it's quiet."

They hurried across the road, but even that short distance in the open made her feel terribly exposed. She ducked into the overgrown bushes with a sigh of relief. Even in the darkness, she could tell that the garden was made up of an astonishing array of plants. Their scents surrounded her, almost dizzying in their intensity. She had to force herself to concentrate on following the narrow path that led to steps up to the front door.

A fine metal chain hung next to the door, and she tugged it quickly. She heard the tinkle of bells inside the house as she hugged Sultavi against her side, hoping she hadn't made a mistake by coming here. Captain Nohta had seemed certain that the Trevelorian scholar would be able to help. He had thrust them through a door concealed in the wall surrounding the compound.

"Go to the scholar. He will help you escape," he had ordered.

"What about you?"

His face had hardened. "I will avenge my lord."

Now the door opened to reveal Opinnas, his brightly colored crest even more disheveled than usual. The Trevelorians were a bird-like race with plump little bodies on long, spindly legs, and his feathers ranged from a deep fuchsia to a very pale pink. He squinted at them through the gold-rimmed spectacles perched on his beak, then breathed a sigh of relief.

"Praise the Goddess! I was just coming to look for you. Come inside. Quickly."

He tugged them into the house, peering anxiously at the street before shutting and locking the door behind them.

"You were expecting us?" she asked suspiciously. Opinnas came to tutor Sultavi three times a week, and he often stayed to teach Joanna about this strange new world. Over the last year she had grown to consider him a friend, but she was all too conscious of how vulnerable they were now.

"One of the kitchen staff managed to escape and sent me a message. He told me what happened."

Sharp black eyes gave Sultavi a sympathetic look as he led the way down the hall into a cluttered kitchen. The whole house was cluttered—a miscellany of objects, books, and scrolls littered every surface, pictures fought for every available inch of wall space, and a colorful array of mismatched fabrics covered the furniture.

The scholar urged them into chairs at the worn wooden table, then bustled around making tea. Sultavi climbed up on Joanna's lap as she watched him, her eyelids drooping.

"How did you get away?" he asked as he placed the cups on the table.

"Captain Nohta got us out of the compound. He said they had been betrayed."

"I told K'herr not to trust T'paja, but he wanted to make peace with him. For her sake," he added softly to Joanna as he distracted Sultavi with a plate of sweet biscuits.

"T'paja? That's the one who was there last night. Aren't they related?"

Opinnas sighed. "Yes. That's the problem. T'paja thinks he can claim leadership of the clan because of his lineage—once he... eliminates his rivals."

"I don't like him," Sultavi piped up, her mouth full of biscuit.

"There is no reason why you should, child." He beckoned to Joanna, and she put Sultavi down and went to join him. "He will be looking for her. I suspect he plans to announce himself as her guardian. You can't let that happen."

"But how can I prevent it?" Fear and frustration warred for dominance. She hated feeling so powerless. "Is there anyone who would take us in?"

"Only those who would seek to take advantage of the child's legacy. You know what this planet is like."

They had discussed it often enough. Alliko was divided into city states, each one ruled over by a separate House. Even though the Houses were no longer constantly at war with each other, they had a long-standing and deep-seated rivalry with each other. Sultavi's heritage—and the fact that she was female—would make her a valuable pawn.

Opinnas clicked his beak together thoughtfully. "You have to get off this planet."

"Off the planet?" The thought of Earth flitted through her mind again, but then she looked at the little girl drawing a finger through her crumbs. "Where would we go?"

"My suggestion is Trevelor. I have family there who would take you in."

"I guess everyone needs slaves." The bitterness escaped before she could prevent it.

His crest flared. "I have told you before that slavery is not allowed in the Confederated Planets."

"That didn't stop the ones who stole us. For that matter, it didn't prevent Lord K'herr from buying me."

"I'm not trying to excuse his actions, but he was only thinking of Sultavi. It could have been far worse."

She sighed and tried to release some of her anger. Opinnas

was right. She had been fed and clothed and treated with a certain amount of courtesy. K'herr had never demanded that she come to his bed, or allowed any other male to do so. But the knowledge that she was a slave had chafed nonetheless.

If they made it to Trevelor, would she really be free at last? A small spark of hope sprang to life in her heart.

"How do we get there?" she asked.

"That might be difficult." He clicked his beak again. "A female and a child traveling alone would attract attention. And not everyone is as law-abiding as they should be..."

"This is the first time I actually wish one of the guards was here," she said regretfully.

"You're right. That's exactly what you need—a guard."

"One of Lord K'herr's?"

He shook his head sadly. "I'm afraid not. From what I was told, no one who was loyal to him survived. I had someone else in mind."

"Who?"

"A mercenary—an old acquaintance of K'herr's. His name is Vanha Pasken, and from what I understand, he is indebted to K'herr."

"Do you know how to find him?"

"I believe so. K'herr gave me his contact information." He gave a rueful smile. "You know what he was like. He always wanted to be prepared."

She didn't really know Lord K'herr at all. They met periodically to discuss Sultavi, but he never talked about himself or asked her personal questions. She wondered now if perhaps he had felt guiltier about her position than she knew.

"I'll contact him." Sharp black eyes looked over at Sultavi, her head drooping. "But it will take time, and you can't stay here."

"Why not?" The thought of going back to racing through

the streets terrified her.

"This is the first place they'll look." He tilted his head. "Well, perhaps not the first place. T'paja never struck me as particularly intelligent. But even he will get around to it."

She supposed he was right. The scholar's trips to the compound were common knowledge.

"Where can we hide until then?"

"In plain sight. Or almost plain sight." His eyes twinkled. "Now drink your tea and I'll take you there."

"I'm bored," Sultavi whined a week later.

"I know, sweetheart," Joanna said as sympathetically as she could. After five days in their tiny hiding place, she understood the little girl's frustration all too well, but she was just as bored and frustrated.

"When is that male going to get here?"

"I don't know." *I wish I did.*

The night they escaped, Opinnas had brought them to this tavern on the edge of the open market. He had assured them that the owner, Rouvi, was completely loyal to Lord K'herr. Rouvi had hidden them in a concealed basement that she was quite sure was used to store illegal liquor. Since then, they had only received two notes from Opinnas. The first had assured her that the message had been sent and to remain hidden. The second had said that help was on the way—but it hadn't provided any details.

The only contact they had had with the outside world was once a day when Rouvi brought them supplies. Afraid to attract attention, his visits had been very brief, but he had told her that the marketplace was still full of Lord T'paja's warriors. None of the merchants were particularly happy about the situation, especially since unlike Lord K'herr, Lord T'paja made no attempt to control his males. He seemed quite happy to let them harass the shopkeepers.

The long delay and the uncertainty of the situation weighed heavily on her. She had barely slept since they arrived. Even when the noise of the tavern above finally died down, she found herself turning over possible fates, each worse than the last.

Fortunately, Sultavi seemed to be able to sleep through anything. Although she'd had several nightmares about the evening they had fled, she always returned to sleep quickly after Joanna comforted her. Unfortunately, sleeping well only added to her daytime restlessness. She was used to busy days with lessons in everything from etiquette to archery, so much so that when Lord K'herr had summoned Joanna for one of his infrequent discussions about his daughter, she had urged him to allow Sultavi more free time.

He had frowned at her, his face as hard as ever. "She must be trained as the future ruler of our House."

"I understand that, but she's still a little girl and she needs time to just... play."

"Play?" He made the word sound like a disease, but finally gave a brief nod. "I will consider the matter."

He had dismissed her without any further concession, but the next day she was provided with an updated schedule that did allow for some additional free time. Despite that, Sultavi had remained busy enough that this enforced period of inactivity was difficult to handle.

Joanna did everything she could think of to keep her occupied. She invented games and told her stories until her throat was sore. In desperation, she had persuaded Rouvi to bring her a deck of the strange Allikan playing cards, and they were now working their way through every card game she could remember.

"Can we look out the window?" Sultavi asked hopefully.

Calling the opening in the outer wall a window was an overstatement. The small rectangle was only about the size of an air conditioner. They had to climb up on the cases stacked against the wall in order to be able to see out—or more accurately, hear out. The opening was covered with a fine metal mesh with a gauze panel behind it, and they could only make out a vague impression of shapes moving around outside.

A heavy wooden shutter could be pulled over the opening. They kept it closed at night so that no trace of light could escape, but Joanna opened it during the day to allow some air into the enclosed space.

Sultavi enjoyed the small glimpse into the outer world, and for that matter, Joanna did too, although she was always nervous at being so close to the market.

"All right," she agreed. "But just for a little while. It will be getting dark soon and we'll have to close the shutter."

Sultavi nodded eagerly and scampered over to the stack of crates. She was halfway up before Joanna could catch her, then climbed into her lap as they settled down on the top crate.

"Mistress Litta is complaining again," Sultavi whispered with a quiet giggle.

The heavyset older female seemed to spend more time complaining about her previous day's purchases than she did making new ones.

"She's never happy," Joanna agreed softly as they listened to her arguing that her marja hadn't been ripe.

"I wish I had some marja. I wouldn't mind if it wasn't ripe."

Sultavi scowled at the window opening, and Joanna gave

her a hug. Her own mouth was watering at the thought of fresh fruit. Their diet had been limited to what Rouvi could bring them without his cook noticing—which tended to be bland crackers and strips of dried meat. She hadn't realized until then how well she had eaten at the compound.

The sound of boots stomping past their window made her shudder, but the familiar voice that followed sent ice through her veins.

"That's Besu," Sultavi whispered, reaching for the panel. "Do you think he's looking for us? Maybe everything is all right after all."

Despite the little girl's optimistic words, Joanna could see the doubt on her face.

"I'm afraid not."

"But he's one of Father's guards!"

And Joanna wouldn't trust him as far as she could throw him. He had come upon her in the gardens one night and, if Nohta hadn't appeared, would have forced himself on her.

Instead, Nohta had hauled him off of her and pushed him away.

"What's wrong with you? You know Lord K'herr gave orders that she was not to be touched."

"Why not?" Besu asked sulkily. "It was just a little fun."

"If you want that kind of fun, go to town."

"Why pay for it when it's available for free here?"

Nohta shook his head in disgust. "You'd risk losing your job because you're too cheap to pay for a whore? Get out of here."

Besu scowled, but stalked away. Nohta looked over at her, his face not unsympathetic.

"Are you all right?"

No. Her hands shook as she clutched her torn gown together across her breasts.

"Yes," she managed.

"Go on back to your quarters. I'll do what I can to keep him away from you, but it would be better to stay out of the gardens at night."

She managed a shaky nod and hurried off before the first tears started to fall. Walking there had been one of the few times when she could escape the reality of her situation, when she could just breathe in the scent of the plants and the enjoy the quiet.

Returning to her room, she took the longest, hottest shower she could stand, trying to wash away the fear and the humiliation and the feeling of being dirty. Then she peeked into the adjoining room. Sultavi was asleep in her enormous bed, her tiny figure dwarfed by the ostentatious surroundings. The little girl was the one bright spot in her captivity, but as much as she loved her, she still longed for her freedom.

And now they were on the run for their lives. So far, freedom was more terrifying than exhilarating.

Sultavi's fingers still hovered over the panel, but Joanna gently drew them away.

"We need to wait and make sure," she whispered as she leaned forward. She could just barely see the guard and his companion, both dressed in Lord T'paja's colors.

"Still no sign of the little bitch?"

The harsh voice came from the other Allikan warrior.

"No," Besu grunted.

"Godsdammit. Lord T'paja is not going to be happy. He needs her to make his claim look legitimate."

"How?"

"He'll claim she's his ward. As soon as she reaches breeding age, he'll mate her and get an heir." The other male shrugged. "Maybe even keep her around to breed a few more if she pleases him."

Besu smirked. "Serves the arrogant little bitch right. So high and mighty. Always ordering me around."

"No sign of the human female either?"

Besu's grin turned to a scowl. "No. But I'm going to find her. I'll teach her not to run."

"Don't damage her too much," the other guard warned. "Lord T'paja said you can have a taste, but human females fetch a pretty profit in the underground markets and he won't be happy if you cut into that."

Besu's scowl darkened. "He said I could have her. That was part of my reward."

The other male laughed and clapped him on the back. "And you will. You just have to give her back. And you'll have enough credits to buy any female who takes your fancy. But you have to find them first."

"I'll find them," Besu muttered as the other guard walked away. "But maybe I won't be handing them over after all."

He too walked off, and Sultavi turned to Joanna, her little face indignant. "He's one of Father's men. And he betrayed him."

"It looks like it."

"Just wait 'til I tell…" Her lip quivered. "I forgot."

"I know, sweetie." Joanna put her arm around the girl and hugged her close.

"What if the person you sent for is like Besu?"

"I'm sure Opinnas wouldn't have suggested contacting him if your father hadn't trusted him," Joanna said as confidently as possible. "Time to close the shutter now," she added. "Can you light the lamp?"

Sultavi nodded eagerly, already distracted from the previous conversation. She hopped down from the pile of crates and found the old-fashioned oil lamp. The cellar didn't have power since Rouvi wished to keep its presence secret. As soon as Sultavi carefully lit the lamp on the lowest setting, Joanna closed the heavy wooden shutter and followed her down. Her hands were shaking, she realized.

They had to get off this planet. If this Vanha didn't show up soon, what were they going to do?

CHAPTER THREE

Craxan Rok'Darian huddled in the darkest corner of the bar, and stared into his drink. He'd never been much of a drinker, but the fiery blue liquid was Vanha's favorite and it seemed only right to be toasting him with it. He could almost hear the old man's voice telling him to just shut up and drink.

If only he were here.

Craxan had known Vanha for most of his life, originally as an arms instructor at his military academy. But then the plague came to his home planet of Ciresia and wiped out his family. Somehow Vanha had managed to get him off Ciresia, even while the officials were rounding up the remaining survivors. Vanha had been the one to train him, to show him the ropes as a mercenary, and to get him in—and out—of trouble.

They had been going their separate ways for the past year after Craxan finally put his foot down and refused to be dragged into another questionably legal enterprise. But they had kept in touch, and the knowledge that Vanha was out in the universe following his own haphazard path had still been there. Then he had received the message that Vanha had been killed and that thread had snapped. He felt as if he'd lost his family all over again.

He had spent most of the last six months tracking down Vanha's killers. The last one had been eliminated today—hence the celebration. Except he didn't feel like celebrating. He felt weary and alone. Without the burning need for revenge that had been driving him, he had no real purpose. The thought of returning to another round of meaningless mercenary jobs held no appeal.

"Hey, Cire." The rough voice interrupted his thoughts.

"Fuck off," he said without looking at the intruder. He was in no mood for conversation.

A big, clawed hand clamped down on his shoulder. "I'm talking to you."

Craxan's warrior reflexes kicked in. He grabbed the hand and twisted it up, while his tail swept out and knocked the other male to his knees. A Skaal, he decided, based on the long fangs and the dark, iridescent scales that shimmered in the dim light of the bar. Not his favorite species, but they weren't as shady as the Vedeckians or as brutal as the Ruijins.

"And I said fuck off." He released the other male and returned to contemplating his drink.

"Godsdammit. I got a message for you."

"What message?"

"You were old Vanha's partner, weren't you?"

The past tense stung, but he turned to have another look at the male climbing cautiously to his feet.

"I was."

"A message came into the spaceport for him. I was hired to deliver it, but when he found out what had happened, he told me to bring it to you instead."

"Who told you?"

The male shrugged. "Don't know. One of those fancy ass Trevelorians. Sent me twenty credits to do it."

He shoved a message tablet towards Craxan.

Craxan eyed it suspiciously, then sighed and took it.

Commander Pasken,

I trust this message finds you well. As you may remember, Lord K'herr rendered his assistance to you some years back in the matter of the Cire youth. He is now in urgent need of your help in a similar matter. Please come to Alliko with all possible speed. You will find me at this location.

An address on Alliko followed, but Craxan was far more interested in the rest of the message. Vanha had needed help from an Allikan? For a Cire youth? It could only have been on his behalf, although he couldn't imagine why a stubborn old bastard like Vanha would have asked anyone else for help.

He certainly didn't bother to ask me for help when he got on the bad side of the Triad, he thought bitterly.

His first instinct was to destroy the message, but if Vanha had truly owed a debt to this Lord K'herr, it was Craxan's responsibility to settle it. And perhaps in the process he could find out more about their past involvement—and any connection to his own history.

"What do you know about this?" he demanded of the Skaal, now seated on the stool next to him. The Skaal was looking at the bottles of liquor behind the bar, rubbing his thumb against his fingers.

"Told you. Just got paid to bring you the message." The male looked down at his hands, then added in a carefully casual tone, "Thought if there was a job involved, you might need some help."

Craxan took another look at him, and this time he recognized the signs of a down-on-his-luck male—the harness that had been mended multiple times, the worn hilt of the knife at his belt, and the attenuated frame that spoke of missed meals. He'd been in the same place once or twice.

"I am not sure what will be required—"

"I'm a mechanic, a good one, and I can fight."

He could see the look of hope on the other male's face, despite his attempt to hide it. *Fuck.* What was he getting himself into?

But he couldn't bring himself to crush the male's hopes. He sighed. "All right. Go find us the first available passage to Alliko. I'll meet you at the spaceport."

He saw the flash of relief on the other male's face before he nodded. "I'm Jed."

"I am Craxan."

THREE DAYS LATER, CRAXAN GAVE THE OLD TREVELORIAN scholar a disbelieving stare.

"You sent an urgent message—in the name of a dead male—because you need a child minder?"

Opinnas simply adjusted his spectacles, unfazed by Craxan's irritation.

"I do not need a child minder. I need an escort for the child."

"It is the same thing," he muttered, but the other male ignored him.

"And I requested the assistance of Commander Pasken

because Lord K'herr had given me to understand that he would assist him. Or, as in this case, his child."

Fuck. He should have followed his first instincts and destroyed the message.

"You do not need me for this. My skills are more... specialized."

"I believe you are overlooking the gravity of the situation. The child—and her companion—are being actively hunted by Lord T'paja. If he finds them, it will result in a life of virtual slavery for the child and actual slavery for her companion."

"Slavery is illegal," he growled.

"Perhaps. But I suspect you know as well as anyone that the Patrol is spread far too thin." Sharp black eyes peered at Craxan, and he had the sudden, uncomfortable feeling that Opinnas was well aware of all of his more questionable activities.

"You cannot get them off the planet yourself?"

"I'm being watched closely, as is anyone who had any dealings with Lord K'herr. And it is not just getting them off the planet. It is getting them safely to Trevelor. If I was to arrange passage for myself and a child, it would immediately be flagged."

Craxan scowled and paced the three steps that were all the small kitchen allowed. His tail lashed angrily, but he did his best to keep it under control to avoid hitting one of the many objects that covered every surface. The entire house made him uncomfortable—it was too small and too cluttered—and it had a cozy feel that reminded him of the home he had lost all those years ago.

"Why did your Lord K'herr think that Vanha would take the job?"

The Trevelorian's feathers fluttered as he shrugged. "I don't know. He told me that they had been acquainted and that he had rendered a service to him."

"Service involving a Cire youth?" He pounced on the statement. "What was it?"

"I don't know. It was some years ago, before the death of his father required him to return to Alliko and assume his duties." Those too sharp eyes were focused on his face again. "But apparently he thought that Commander Pasken would be grateful enough to perform a similar act."

There was that phrase again, but it took on new significance now that he knew the nature of the job. Was it possible that Lord K'herr had meant it literally?

The days after his family died had been a confused blur of rage and mourning. Then the Ciresian High Council had sent out orders for the survivors to gather under their "protection," but it had been the last thing he wanted to do. Somehow, Vanha had spirited him onto a spaceship and off of the planet. Could that have been with Lord K'herr's assistance?

He sighed and rubbed the back of his neck. In the end, he supposed it made little difference. It was a debt of honor and he would fulfill it. There was only one problem...

"What are you paying for the job?"

The other male's beak clicked. "You expect to be paid? For fulfilling a debt of honor?"

"Yes," he said firmly, fighting back an immediate feeling of guilt.

His own funds were almost gone. The hunt for Vanha's killers had used up most of his limited savings, and the flight here had been more expensive than he had anticipated. Fortunately, Jed had been able to fill in for one of the ship's mechanics a few times and lessened the cost of his passage.

"Oh dear. I didn't take that into consideration." The feathered crest bobbed anxiously. "I have very few credits on hand

and raising more would take time. Time I'm not sure that we have."

"Passage on a ship is not free," he reminded the other male, already resigned to the fact that he would not be getting paid. It would not be the first time. The reason his savings had been so limited in the first place was his unfortunate tendency to take on quixotic missions.

"How much would you need?"

"For three—no, four people?" He wasn't going to leave Jed stranded on this planet. "At least a thousand credits."

The sum made the scholar's eyes widen, then his feathers drooped.

"I don't have access to that much. I have some savings, but they are deposited on Trevelor. It could take days to arrange for the transfer. I do have a few things I could sell in a hurry." He gestured rather vaguely at the miscellaneous objects surrounding them. "But I would be lucky to raise one tenth of that."

Craxan's tail twitched unhappily. Perhaps he had made the wrong decision in coming here. He was out of funds, he hadn't received any answers, and he had an unwanted obligation to fulfill.

"How long will it take to sell them?"

The scholar looked out at the gathering darkness. "A few hours. Fortunately, the quick sale brokers are open late to accommodate the late-night gamblers."

"Very well. See how much you can raise and I will make inquiries at the spaceport."

"You mean you'll do it?" Opinnas asked eagerly.

"Yes." He had an obligation to Vanha's memory, but more than that – he couldn't leave a child to be victimized.

By the time all of the arrangements were made, it was long after midnight. *But perhaps that is for the best*, Craxan thought as he followed Opinnas through the dark streets. Despite the Trevelorian's ungainly body, he moved with surprising stealth, slipping silently from one shadowed area to another.

They slipped down a narrow alley, then into another, even narrower space behind several taverns. The area was littered with empty cases and barrels, and there was an overwhelming stench of stale beer and rotten food. His sensitive scent receptors quivered with disgust, but it wasn't the first time, nor he suspected the last time, that he had been exposed to such unpleasantness.

"Wait here and keep watch," Opinnas muttered, then disappeared through the back door of the closest tavern.

Craxan sighed and eyed the mouth of the alley warily. It had been a frantic few hours. Once again, Jed had been able to use his connections to find a ship heading in the right direction. The captain had taken him on as a temporary crew member readily enough, but he hadn't been as enthusiastic about Craxan.

Captain Merios had leaned against the open ramp of his ship and studied Craxan, rubbing his chin thoughtfully. Like all Kissat males, he was carefully groomed, his dark fur smooth and shining, and his small horns polished.

"Got any skills?"

Craxan let his hand rest on the knife in his belt. "Enough."

The captain snorted. "Don't need security on my ship. Everyone works—" His gaze wandered over to Jed. "And behaves themselves, or they get tossed out the airlock."

The casual brutality of the statement would have appalled him once. He'd seen enough now to know that you couldn't let one person's weakness endanger everyone else.

"I am strong and willing to work."

"Nah. Got enough dumb labor." He jerked a thumb at a young Vaivan male, struggling to carry an oversized basket up the ramp. The boy was already tall, but he was painfully thin, his muscles not yet catching up to the promise of his size. From the pale orange tint to his scales he had only just reached maturity.

"But there is one thing," the captain said thoughtfully. "Gotta make a stop on Driguera. Take on some new cargo. I'm not exactly welcome there."

"Then why are you going back?" He asked before he could stop himself. *Fuck.* He knew better than to ask questions.

The captain didn't seem offended. He shrugged. "Cargo is worth my while. But I could have some... difficulty retrieving it. You come along with me, make sure we make it safely there—and back to the ship—and I'll give you a family cabin all the way to Trevelor."

Sharing a single cabin with the child and her companion was the last thing he wanted to do, especially since he suspected it would be ridiculously small.

"How many bunks?" he asked.

Unexpectedly shrewd eyes studied Craxan's face. "Two. One for the child and one for you and your... mate."

Craxan had told him he was seeking passage for himself and his mate and child. From the skepticism in the captain's voice, he had his doubts about the story. Hardly surprising since the Cire were known for their devotion to their females. To the Cire females who no longer existed. The plague had robbed his race of all hope for the future when it took their females. The familiar pang made his chest ache but he shoved it aside. The captain could be as suspicious as he liked, but as long as he didn't interfere, Craxan didn't care.

But only two bunks? Not the most desirable arrangements. The companion would just have to sleep on the floor, he decided.

"Done."

"Food's not included. Bring your own or pay for it on board."

He nodded again, hoping that Opinnas had at least managed to secure enough funds to cover their meals.

"We leave at first light. If you're not on board, I won't wait." The captain had shot another look at Jed, then strolled up the ramp.

Craxan could hear him yelling at his young crew member as he turned to Jed.

"Are you sure he is trustworthy?"

"He has a reputation for keeping his word." The other male shrugged. "But I don't trust anybody."

"Not even me?" he asked satirically.

To his surprise, Jed shook his head. "I trust you."

"Why?"

"You have a reputation too. And the fact that you're doing this? You didn't have to follow up on some supposed debt you didn't know anything about."

Craxan looked away uncomfortably. "I did not have anything else to do."

"Yeah. If you say so."

Craxan had ended the discussion, taking Jed back to the Trevelorian's house with him. When Opinnas returned with an unfortunately small number of credits, Craxan had sent Jed off to purchase some basic supplies while he accompanied the other male to pick up his charges.

As he stood in the alley now, waiting, he wondered if it had been foolish to entrust Jed with the funds. They had formed the foundations of a friendship on the voyage here but, like Jed, his trust was not easily won.

The sound of a door opening distracted him from his thoughts. The professor stepped into the alley, accompanied by a small figure in a hooded cloak clutching the hand of a child dressed in an oversized dark shirt. At the same time, a hint of deliciously sweet fragrance cut through the stench of the alley. He had never smelled anything quite so enticing. The tip of his tail flicked restlessly.

"My dear, this is Craxan. Craxan, this is Joanna and Sultavi."

He heard a startled breath and looked down to see the child's companion—Joanna—staring up at him. Even in the dim light of the alley, he could see delicate features and smooth pale skin. Big, brown eyes studied him in return, and then a small pink tongue swept nervously across a plump lower lip. Female. *Very female*, he amended, unable to resist a quick sweep down her body. The cloak did not completely obscure her generous curves.

For some reason, he had assumed that the child's companion would be a grim older female. A guard. *Not a soft, desirable*—his thoughts came to an abrupt halt.

"I do not think that this will work."

"Why not?" Opinnas asked.

"You can't help us?" Joanna asked.

Her voice was low and pleasing, despite her obvious distress. His immediate instinct was to comfort her, but he had to resist the urge. She deserved far more than an uncertain passage on a cargo ship of questionable repute.

"Why is your tail doing that?" the child asked, her eyes wide and innocent.

He looked down to find his tail stroking the impossibly soft skin of the female's wrist soothingly. *Fuck.* He snatched it back.

"It was an... apology."

The female was still staring at him, blunt little teeth worrying that tempting lower lip. "Why can't you help us?"

"I was only able to procure one cabin." A small cabin that she would fill with her irresistible fragrance, where he would be unable to avoid brushing up against those luscious curves... To his complete and utter shock, his cock jerked. One of the crueler ironies surrounding the loss of their females was that the remaining males were incapable of complete sexual pleasure. Pleasure that could only come during intercourse with a true mate. It had been many years since he'd even attempted to find pleasure with a female.

"You're apologizing again," the female said.

He yanked his tail back under control.

"One cabin is fine," she added, although he could hear the doubt in her voice. "At least we would be away from this planet."

And at risk from every type of scum—those who would only see her as valuable merchandise. He remembered the Trevelorian's earlier words and his own blithe denial of the threat of slavery, but he knew it existed. At the thought of this soft, beautiful female subject to those horrors, he growled.

Her eyes widened, and her sweet scent increased.

"Did you just growl?"

Unwilling to lie, he chose not to answer, looking at Opinnas instead. "You know how dangerous this could be."

"Which is why you are needed." The Trevelorian's eyes dropped to where Craxan's tail was now circling the female's wrist. "I believe you are the perfect male for the job."

A small hand covered his tail as she looked up at him beseechingly. "Please, Craxan. You're our only hope."

At the sound of his name on her lips and the feel of her skin as she touched him, his cock stiffened into a full, aching erection. *Fuck.* This was going to be an excruciating trip—and he could no more refuse her than he could stop breathing.

"Very well."

CHAPTER FOUR

Joanna breathed a sigh of relief as the massive alien nodded. She had never seen anyone quite like him before, neither amongst the aliens she had seen at the slave auction nor the ones who frequented the market. His skin was patterned in shades of rich green, with darker ridges that led up over a well-shaped head. He had a wide, lipless mouth and a flat nose, but his features were oddly compelling, as were the black eyes fastened so intently on her face.

The dark shirt and pants he was wearing clung to acres of muscles, from impossibly broad shoulders to narrow hips and thick thighs and... She quickly jerked her eyes away, but she was quite sure she had seen an equally massive bulge. Oh, Lord—and she was going to be sharing a cabin with him? She should be terrified, but instead she felt a completely unexpected warmth low in her stomach.

Her hand automatically patted the tail still wrapped around her wrist, noticing for the first time that it was covered with small nubs that felt intriguingly rough against her skin. *I wonder if he's like that all over,* she thought, then felt the heat rise to her cheeks.

What is wrong with me?

Sultavi tugged on her sleeve, and she turned to her, grateful for the distraction. "What is it, sweetheart?"

"I'm tired. Will you carry me?"

"Of course." She bent to pick her up, but as she straightened, her exhaustion caught up with her and she stumbled.

Craxan's tail immediately wrapped around her waist, supporting them both.

"She is too heavy for you."

"No, she's not. I'm just a little tired."

He frowned at her. "If you will permit... If she will permit..."

Before she could respond, he bent down to look at Sultavi. "Will you allow me to carry you? Your... Joanna is weary."

Sultavi buried her head in Joanna's neck, and she bit back a sigh. Not that she normally minded, but weariness was dragging at her. Then the little girl peeked back at Craxan.

"Are you going to betray us?"

He looked shocked, then solemnly shook his head. "By Granthar's Hammer, I swear you are safe with me."

Purple eyes studied black eyes, then Sultavi nodded. "You may carry me."

Joanna saw Craxan's mouth curve at the regal note in the little girl's voice, but he lifted her carefully into his arms. She looked impossibly small against that broad chest, but she smiled happily.

"We should leave now," Craxan said and Opinnas nodded.

The scholar led the way, with Joanna behind him and Craxan forming the rear guard. She was overwhelmingly conscious of his presence behind her, and finally darted a quick look over her shoulder. As she suspected, he was watching her, his face full of masculine appreciation. Ignoring her pleasant little flutter of excitement in response, she looked at Sultavi. Her head was tucked against his neck, her eyes closed.

"Is she asleep?" she whispered.

"No," Sultavi mumbled sleepily, and they both smiled.

Then his gaze lifted over her head and his face hardened into an almost unrecognizable mask.

"Hold her," he ordered, passing her the girl and stepping in front of both of them.

Opinnas had come to a halt, she realized, just as they reached the plaza in front of the spaceport. A plaza with two Allikan guards leaning against the entrance pillars. They looked neither alert nor interested, but there was no way their party could cross the space without being seen.

"Is there another way inside?" Craxan asked quietly.

"There's a fence around the perimeter. You could possibly scale it..."

Craxan waved at the faint line of light along the horizon indicating the coming dawn. "No time."

"I should have realized that there would be someone here, even at this time," Opinnas said apologetically.

Joanna's heart skipped a beat. They were so close.

"I'm scared," Sultavi whispered.

"I know, sweetheart."

She tightened her arms around the warm little body, then made her decision.

"Take her and head for the ship. I'll distract them." Both of the males looked so appalled that she almost giggled hysterically. "I'm sure I'll be fine—you both said that I was valuable. And Tavi will be safe."

"No!" Sultavi's arms wrapped around her neck. "You can't leave me."

She hugged her back, her heart breaking, but she couldn't see any other way.

"Unacceptable," Craxan pronounced, as if that resolved the matter.

"Do you have an alternative?"

He put his hand on his blaster, and she glared at him. "All that would do is bring all the other guards running."

"Your idea has merit, my dear." Opinnas ignored Craxan's growl. "Except I will provide the distraction. Craxan can then take them by surprise and, err, dispatch them silently."

"Can you do that?" she asked the big alien.

"Yes." He glanced at the brightening horizon. "But it will have to be fast. I will head to that side."

Without another word, he vanished back into the streets. Her throat felt curiously tight as she turned back to Opinnas.

"Are you sure about this?"

He peered at her over his spectacles. "Of course."

Slipping off his own cloak, he handed it to her. "Wrap this around Sultavi so her features can't be seen."

Before she could respond, he staggered out into the plaza. The guards immediately snapped to attention as he headed for them, singing an extremely dirty song, loudly and off key. One of the guards shook his head, and the other one grinned.

And then Craxan was there. He seemed to emerge out of the shadows, his big body moving with a grace and speed that belied his size. His tail swept out, knocking one guard to his knees, only to have Craxan deliver a hammer-like blow to the back of his skull. He dropped like a stone. The other guard started to turn, but he was too late. Craxan yanked his arm up behind him, and the sharp crack echoed through the quiet plaza. Another blow and the second guard dropped.

The whole thing had taken less than thirty seconds.

She stared at the fallen bodies, stunned, dismayed, and more than a little turned on.

"He's better than Lutta," Sultavi said dispassionately. Lutta was the guard teaching her self-defense.

"Hurry!" The call from Opinnas snapped Joanna out of her shock, and she took off at a run.

Craxan met her halfway, lifting her and Sultavi into his arms without even breaking stride. As he headed for the cargo gate, she turned and waved at Opinnas.

"Thank you!"

"Take care of yourself and the child."

His voice faded as Craxan ducked through the gate and started across the landing field.

"I can walk," she offered.

He glanced down at her, his eyes warm and amused. "No time. And I enjoy carrying you."

All righty then.

Peering over her shoulder, she saw they were heading for the most dilapidated-looking ship she had ever seen.

"Can that thing even fly?" she asked.

"Don't let it fool you. The captain keeps it that way on purpose." His amusement faded. "Now cover as much of yourself and the child as you can. I want to keep your identities concealed for as long as possible."

She pulled the hood of her cloak down over her face, then arranged the one Opinnas had given her so that nothing could be seen of Sultavi. The little girl didn't protest, half-asleep again.

Her face was pressed against Craxan's neck, and she could feel the intriguing texture of his skin against her cheek. It appeared those tantalizing little nubs did cover his whole body. She took a deep breath. Mmm. He smelled so good, like dark, bittersweet chocolate. Did he taste like chocolate as well?

Giving in to a sudden, completely irrational impulse, she flicked her tongue across his skin.

He shuddered, then tensed.

"Cutting it pretty close, aren't you? Never thought I'd see the day when an unreliable soak like Jed would be more dependable than a Cire warrior."

She didn't recognize the new voice, but it had a lazy, mocking quality that irritated her.

"I had business to conclude."

"I see. Like hiding your family?" the stranger asked sardonically.

Craxan growled, and she felt that one reverberate inside her core.

"No one looks at my mate, Merios."

"Interesting. That almost sounded like a possessive Cire male." Merios said thoughtfully. "But we all know that's impossible, don't we?"

"Just fly the damn ship out of here and stop worrying about my life."

"Whatever you say, honored guest." Definitely mocking. "Your cabin is the third one on the right. Second level."

Craxan started walking again without another word. She had a hard time restraining herself from trying to peek at the owner of the annoying voice, but she managed. Craxan climbed a flight of stairs, and she heard a door slide open. He stepped inside, but didn't immediately put her down. His body was still rigid, and she was just about to ask what was wrong when she felt the vibration. The ship was taking off.

Craxan's muscles unlocked, and he brushed the cloak away from her face.

"We have left the surface," he said and smiled.

He leaned over to put her down, and she gave into another impulse and brushed her lips across his cheek. For a second, his muscles turned rigid again, then he continued bending down until her feet touched the floor. Her cheeks heating, she tried to take a step back and hit the wall.

She could feel her blush increasing as she stumbled, and Craxan gently took Sultavi away from her.

She rubbed her head and looked around. He certainly hadn't been kidding when he said it would be a tiny cabin. If she extended her arms, she suspected she could touch both walls at the same time. A narrow bench ran along one wall, while the other wall had some odd-looking panels. Everything was a dingy white—not dirty, exactly, but worn from age and casual maintenance.

Her eyes went back to the bench, upholstered in what looked like patched vinyl. Was that intended to be the bed? She wasn't even sure it was wide enough for her, let alone the three of them.

"Umm, is that where we're supposed to sleep?"

Craxan shook his head, then reached over her to manipulate a wall panel. A second bench opened higher in the wall, this one clearly intended as a bed despite its narrow size. He gently placed Sultavi into it. She barely stirred.

Which left the bottom bench for the two of them. She eyed it uncertainly. Should she offer to sleep on the floor?

Before she could speak, Craxan pressed another button and the bench slid across the room as the back dropped down next to it, leaving only a narrow pathway between the bed and the wall. The resulting surface was not much wider than a twin bed, but it looked infinitely more comfortable than the bench. Two thin pillows and two flimsy blankets had been stored behind the back, and Craxan reached across the bed to grab them and place them on the bench.

"You should get some sleep," he said.

"But what about you?"

"I need to go check on my companion."

"Companion?" Did he mean a girlfriend? And why did that thought distress her? She barely knew the man—male.

"Are you going to stay with her—them?" The question popped out before she could stop it.

He tilted his head, studying her face, then his tail patted her hand again. Somehow she hadn't realized it was encircling her wrist once more.

"No. Jed is in a crew bunk. I just want to make sure that he is safely on board and find out what supplies he acquired." A flash of what looked like worry crossed the alien features. "You should rest," he continued. "I will return later."

He took the one small step to the door, then turned back. "The door is keyed to my retinal pattern. No one else can enter. You are both safe."

She nodded, and his tail tightened briefly before slipping away, leaving her wrist feeling oddly cold and bare. The door slid closed behind him with a quiet click, and she sank down on the bunk.

After the fear of the past week, she supposed she should feel relieved, but instead she only felt curiously numb. Everything had happened so quickly. From leaving the confined basement to the terrifying run through the streets to another confined space. *Even smaller this time*, she thought wearily. And she hadn't thought to ask about bathroom facilities.

One of the panels on the opposite wall was roughly the size of a door, and with a little experimentation she managed to slide it open. The tiny bathroom reminded her uncomfortably of the bathroom on the slave ship—a minuscule sink, a toilet with a disturbing resemblance to an airline toilet, and an overhead fixture that released a liquid that was most definitely not water, but nonetheless effective. With a sigh, she stepped inside and turned on the shower. After their time in the tavern basement with its extremely limited facilities, she was desperate to feel clean again.

She didn't even bother removing her clothes—they were as dirty as the rest of her. The soap dispenser used the same disinfectant soap as the slave ship, and she sighed again. What she wouldn't give to be back in the big bathtub in her apartment with an array of sweet-smelling bath products and the candles lining the window sill. If slavery was illegal, she was a free woman again and, maybe now that she was away from Alliko it might be possible to return to Earth. But then she thought of the little girl sleeping in the upper bunk.

No, Earth and her life there was behind her now. She just needed to come up with a plan to support the two of them.

The flow of liquid was replaced with the blast of hot air that served in place of a towel. She already knew it wouldn't work on her clothing, so she stripped off the shirt and pants, turning around until her body was relatively dry.

When she peeked out into the cabin, Craxan had not returned, so she grabbed one of the thin sheets and wrapped it around herself before hanging her clothes from the hooks she discovered behind another panel. The sheet was coarse and scratchy, but it seemed clean enough, and she sank down on the bed as exhaustion overcame her.

She stacked the two thin pillows under her head and tried to think of how she could make a living, but her thoughts kept straying to the big green alien. *Maybe he would have a suggestion,* she thought, but as she drifted off to sleep all she could think about was how safe she had felt cradled in his arms.

CHAPTER FIVE

Craxan rubbed his eyes wearily as he returned to his cabin. He had checked on Jed and found the other male was not only safely on board, but had managed to stretch their limited funds to acquire a surprising quantity of supplies. Since Jed's shift wasn't due to start for a few hours, they had gone to the ship's exercise room to train. He had hoped that the exercise would relieve some of the lingering adrenaline from the encounter with the guards, not to mention his body's uncontrollable reaction to the female now occupying their cabin.

Instead, he had spent the entire time fighting the urge to return to her. Visions of her sleeping in their bed—*her* bed—kept flashing through his head. He even made a mistake stupid enough to allow Jed to flip him. He wasn't sure which of them was more surprised, but then he heard Merios laugh as he strolled into the room.

"My, my. You are destroying all my illusions. The Cire have such an impressive reputation as warriors, and yet you can be defeated by a drunken Skaal." He gave Jed a derogatory glance. "And despite the touching stories of your race's sole devotion to your Cire mates, you seem quite satisfied with another. Tell me, who is she?"

"None of your business," he growled.

"Really? I find that even more intriguing." The captain's teeth flashed in what could not be called a smile. "But she will need to leave the cabin at some point—or are you going to keep her confined there for the entire trip?"

He didn't bother answering, turning back to Jed. Spurred on by his frustration, he flipped the other male in three quick brutal moves.

The captain laughed again. "If you damage one of my crew members, there will be penalties."

With that parting shot, he left and Craxan turned back to Jed, reaching down a hand to help the other male to his feet.

"I apologize. I know better than to let someone like Merios goad me."

Jed grinned at him, seemingly unperturbed. "Females have that effect on a male."

"She's not my female," he said, reminding himself as much as the other male, but the words felt wrong in his mouth.

"She is for the purposes of this trip," Jed reminded him. He gave Craxan a disturbingly penetrating look, but didn't add anything else. Instead, he walked to the edge of the mats and began toweling off. "I have to get ready for my shift. You should transfer the supplies to your own locker."

"What about you?"

"For all his bluster, Merios feeds his crew extremely well. I'm fine."

"I suspect this is not the type of job you had in mind when you sought to accompany me."

Jed shrugged. "I needed a chance. This suits me well enough." He shot a quick look at Craxan. "And Merios wouldn't have hired me if he hadn't known you were coming along."

So the captain's seeming reluctance had been an act. Somehow, he wasn't surprised. His mention of Driguera had been a little too casual.

"Why is that?" he asked. "You have the skills to be more than just a low-level mechanic."

"I was an engineer once." The other male looked away, rubbing his towel back and forth over his bare arms. Just as Craxan had decided not to press the matter, Jed spoke again. "My father was a drinker. He gave me my first drink when I was five. By the time I made it to engineer, I was starting with ale in the morning and moving on to liquor by midday. I thought I had it under control, even when I needed a shot of something in my tea just to start the day. But then I made a mistake and people died."

The other male's face was haunted, staring back into the past, before he finally shook his head.

"Now I have a reputation. A bad one. You heard Merios—he still thinks I'm a drunk."

"Are you?"

Jed looked him directly in the eye. "I haven't touched a drop in four hundred and eighty-two days. But I will always be a drinker."

Craxan nodded, then picked up his own towel.

"That's it?" Jed asked, "No recriminations? No desire to disassociate yourself from me?"

"We all make mistakes." If he hadn't let his stupid sense of morality get the better of him, then he would have been there when those bastards came after Vanha.

Jed reached over and clasped his forearm. "I won't let you down."

"It is more important that you do not let yourself down."

The other male dipped his head in acknowledgment, and they parted ways.

Craxan could no longer prevent himself from returning to the cabin. His tail twitched eagerly as he approached, but he resolved to keep it under control. He had no business touching a female who did not belong to him, even though she did not seem disturbed by his touch.

As soon as he opened the door, her scent surrounded him, thick in the humid air. She must have taken a shower, and the thought of her naked body combined with her delectable fragrance caused an immediate response from his cock. Apparently neither his tail nor his cock were inclined to obey his wishes.

Or his eyes, seeking her out immediately where she lay sprawled in slumber on the lower bunk. The overhead lights caught sparks of gold in her soft brown hair. One of the meager blankets was wrapped around her, but it had slipped down to expose the curve of a pale, fragile shoulder. The clothes she had been wearing were hanging on the wall, and he realized she must be naked beneath the thin cloth. His cock jerked again, and he decided that he had best return to the training room for more exercise.

"I remember you." The soft little voice jerked him out of his abstraction, and he looked up to see two purple eyes sparkling at him from the upper bunk. Sultavi was awake.

"What do you remember?" he asked equally quietly, reluctant to awake his—*the*—sleeping female.

"You said you wouldn't betray us."

He nodded, his chest aching at the trust on the innocent little face. "I would never betray you."

"Besu betrayed us. My father is dead."

Or perhaps not so innocent.

"I am sorry about that."

Her lips quivered. "I didn't see Father much, but I miss him."

"I missed my father as well after he died."

How much he had missed the kind older male. Then Vanha had assumed the role. The two were very different, but he had loved them both. And lost them both. *Never again*, he reminded himself as his chest ached.

Sultavi nodded solemnly, then her expression changed and she gave him a beseeching look.

"I want to get down now. I've been waiting and waiting, but Miss Joanna won't wake up."

"I think she was very tired." He started to lean over the bottom bunk to lift her down, and she launched herself at him. She didn't seem to have any doubt that he would catch her. Two tiny arms curved around his neck as she hugged him, and his heart melted.

"I'm glad you came for us," she whispered.

His tail automatically came up to pat her back. "I am too," he agreed.

And he was, he realized. Protecting Joanna and Sultavi made him feel more complete than he had felt since Vanha died, like he had a family again.

No. He couldn't go there. He couldn't risk losing another family. He was here to do a job and then he would let them go.

"Now that you are awake, what do you want to do?" he asked, trying to distract himself, and then realized he had made a mistake. He had no idea what to do with a small child.

"I'm hungry," she announced.

Shame immediately washed over him as he stared at her in appalled horror. Why had he not considered that? A child in his care should never go hungry.

"I will remedy that at once," he promised, then realized that in his haste to return to the cabin, he had not brought any of the supplies with him. "Although I am afraid you will have to wait, just a very short time, while I obtain something for you to eat."

Big eyes gave him a pitiful look. "I want to go with you."

He started to refuse, then reconsidered. Now that they were in space, she should be free from her father's enemies. And since he had already declared her as his child, it would only be natural that she should accompany him. The lockers were only one level below them, and they were unlikely to run into any members of the small crew. But just in case...

"If we should encounter anyone else, they will think that you are my child," he warned her.

She giggled. "But you're green."

"That does not matter."

Those big purple eyes studied his face. "They think you're my father?"

"Yes."

"Does that mean I have to call you Father?"

"Is that what you called your parent?" When she nodded, her eyes sorrowful, he considered the matter. "Then perhaps another name would be best. What do you think of Papa?"

She tilted her head, then gave a satisfied nod. "I like it. Does that mean I can call Miss Joanna 'Mama?'"

He looked down at the sleeping female, remembering her fierce devotion to the child and her offer to sacrifice herself so that Sultavi could go free.

"You can ask her when she wakes up, but I think she would like that very much."

"Okay, Papa."

His chest ached at the words he had never thought to hear. But this was a job, he reminded himself, and right now, he needed to provide for his young... daughter.

"Now I will feed you," he promised.

She gave an excited squeal, quickly hushed, and threw her

arms around his neck again. He fought back a smile as he slipped out of the cabin and locked the door behind him.

Halfway down the corridor, the young Vaivan appeared, carrying a mop bucket. He flinched at the sight of Craxan and drew back against the wall to let him pass.

"Hello," Sultavi said cheerfully. "I'm Sultavi, and this is my *papa*. Who are you?"

The young male shot a doubtful glance at Craxan and mumbled something unintelligible.

"I can't hear you," Sultavi said impatiently.

"I'm Yengik." He kept his eyes downcast as he spoke.

"Hello, Yengik. My papa is taking me to get something to eat."

"Oh." Yengik looked even more hesitant, but pointed back the way they had come. "The galley is in that direction."

"I have supplies in my locker," he said firmly. He had no intention of associating with the rest of the crew any more than necessary.

"Oh." The young male bent over and picked up the bucket again, and Craxan's curiosity got the better of him.

"Do you not have cleaning bots on this ship?" he asked.

"Y... yes." Yengik ducked his head. "But Captain Merios told me to do it this way after he found me working on a robobeast."

"A robobeast? I love those!" Sultavi exclaimed.

A shy smile crossed the boy's face. "You can have it when I'm finished. If it's all right with your father," he added quickly, his smile fading.

"Please, Papa," Sultavi begged.

He was no match for two pairs of hopeful eyes. "Very well. Now you must be about your duties, and I must feed my child."

Yengik immediately rushed off.

"I like him," Sultavi announced.

"I do too." Despite Yengik's obvious shyness - no doubt worsened by the way Merios treated him. He seemed so young, and yet Craxan suspected that he was the same age Craxan had been when he had escaped his dying planet. Had he been as awkward and ungainly, he wondered.

They met no one else on the way to the storage lockers, and he breathed a sigh of relief. Sultavi chose a packet of sweet biscuits and nibbled on them happily while he gathered a selection to take back to Joanna.

"Do you have any juice?" Sultavi asked, her mouth full of biscuit.

"I am afraid not."

"There is juice in the galley." The mocking voice was unmistakable, and he turned around to see Merios lounging against the door frame.

"We have other beverages," he said firmly.

"Indeed? But why deny the child?"

The captain strolled into the room, then bent down in front of Sultavi. Every muscle in Craxan's body tensed, but he didn't want to start a fight so close to the child.

"Hello, little one. What's your name?" The captain's voice was surprisingly soft.

"I'm Sultavi." She smiled proudly. "And that's my papa."

"Indeed?" Merios raised a skeptical eyebrow, but didn't contradict her. "Since your... father won't get you any juice, how about a sweet?"

The captain showed her his empty palm, then closed his fist. When he opened it again, a collection of small sweets covered the dark fur. Sultavi's eyes widened.

"How did you do that?"

"Magic," Merios said lightly. "Especially for you."

She reached out her hand, then stopped and looked up at him. "Can I have them, Papa?"

He couldn't resist her hopeful expression. "Yes, but you must save them for later."

"How very parental." Merios rose to his feet, brushing away an imaginary speck of dust from his immaculate jacket. "I am almost convinced."

Craxan gritted his teeth, refusing to respond.

"And your mate?" the captain continued.

"Mama's asleep," Sultavi volunteered. "We're getting her breakfast."

"Most... appetizing." Merios cast a disparaging glance at the collection of dried foods. "Some of those will require heating. You may use the galley if you wish. I won't even charge you for it."

He wanted to throw the offer back in the other male's face, but Merios was correct. Some of the items would be more palatable if heated.

"Perhaps," he said grudgingly.

"Of course, the galley is Rissta's domain," Merios added thoughtfully.

Craxan frowned at him. Was that some kind of veiled threat?

The captain laughed at his expression and shook his head. "I will let you experience that pleasure for yourself." He turned back to Sultavi, his expression softening. "Goodbye, little one."

"I like him too," Sultavi announced as the captain disappeared.

He wanted to object, but she smiled up at him so innocently that he didn't have the heart.

"He seemed to like you too," he said truthfully. "Now let us go and see if your mama is awake."

As soon as he opened the cabin door, he knew he was in trouble. A wide awake and very angry female advanced on him.

CHAPTER SIX

Joanna snatched Sultavi out of Craxan's arms. Tears threatened, both from anger and relief. She had woken up alone, feeling surprisingly rested, only to discover that Sultavi was no longer in the cabin. Horrific scenarios tumbled through her mind as she hastily pulled on her still damp clothing. A distant part of her mind told her that it would be foolish to leave the cabin, but her urgency to find the little girl drove her to the door, only to find out that it was locked.

When Craxan had said that it was keyed to his retinal scan, she had assumed he meant to keep others out. She hadn't realized he meant to keep her trapped as well. How could she have been so foolish as to put her trust in him? Just because he was big and strong and had treated both of them with kindness didn't mean that she could let down her guard.

She wanted to bang on the door, to scream for help, but if it was truly keyed to him, all it would do was attract unwanted attention. Instead, she closed the bunk and paced the small length of the cabin angrily, plotting increasingly more improbable plans for revenge.

Now Sultavi squirmed in her arms, and she realized she was holding her too tightly.

"Sorry, sweetheart." She relaxed her grip even as she glared at Craxan. "How could you do that? I woke up and didn't know where she was—or where you were. Why didn't you tell me you were taking her?"

"You were sleeping. We did not want to disturb you." His tail tried to pat her wrist and she angrily brushed it away.

"You could at least have left me a note."

"You can read Galactic standard?"

His surprise only added to her anger.

"Of course I can. I'm an educated woman." Opinnas had taught her over the past year.

He bowed his head. "I apologize. I should not have taken the child away from you without your knowledge."

His obvious sincerity blunted her anger, but she couldn't entirely let it go.

"And what makes you think it's safe for her to leave the cabin?"

Sultavi had been watching them both anxiously, her eyes flicking between their faces.

"It was fun," she said now. "Yengik said he would make me a robobeast and the captain gave me some sweets. But I can't have them until later," she added with a resigned sigh.

Joanna closed her eyes in despair. Apparently Sultavi's identity was no longer secret.

Craxan's tail curved comfortably around her wrist again, and this time she let it stay.

"I have claimed her as my daughter," he reminded her. "And I do not believe there is anyone on board who would wish her harm."

"Are you sure?"

"It is my job—my honor—to protect you both." Those black

eyes fastened intently on her face. "I will never let you come to harm."

She sighed and released the rest of her anger as she put Sultavi down. "All right. But I think we need to work on our communication skills."

"Of course. I am willing to learn anything you wish to teach me."

The words were innocent enough, but the warmth in his eyes was not. Several entirely inappropriate lessons sprang to mind and her nipples tingled, thrusting at the damp silk of her top. His eyes focused there with an almost tangible heat. The air between them seemed to thicken, until Sultavi spoke and broke the spell.

"Are we going to eat now?"

Craxan immediately looked appalled. "Did I not provide sufficient food earlier?"

"That was breakfast." She gave him a sunny smile. "Now it's time for lunch."

The mention of food made Joanna realize just how hungry she was, and her stomach growled. Craxan looked even more horrified.

He's disgusted because my body needs food?

"I am deeply sorry for my neglect," he said, and she relaxed, patting his tail. He gave a muffled groan, and she realized he must be really upset.

"Don't worry, Craxan. It's been a hectic time."

"That is no excuse." He urged her to a seat on the bench with Sultavi beside her, then opened one of the wall panels to reveal a table which folded out in front of them. He proceeded to cover the surface with a wide selection of food packets. "I was not sure what you would enjoy."

"That is quite a selection." *And none of them are familiar.*

"Unfortunately, some of them would be better if they were heated," he added apologetically.

"You mean a kitchen isn't going to pop out of the magic wall?" she teased.

He grinned, a surprisingly charming grin despite the flash of fangs, and she realized it was the first time she had seen him smile so freely.

"The captain said we could use his galley, Mama. Isn't that like a kitchen?" Sultavi asked, and Joanna froze.

"You called me Mama," she whispered, her eyes filling with tears. As much as she thought of Tavi as her child, she hadn't wanted to infringe on the memory of the female who had given birth to her. Not to mention that Lord K'herr would never have permitted his daughter to express that sentiment towards a slave.

"Is that all right?" Those big purple eyes looked up at her anxiously. "I forgot that Papa said I should ask you first."

"Of course it's all right. I would love for you to call me that." She hugged the little girl, fighting back the tears. Then the rest of her words penetrated. "Papa?"

Craxan shrugged uncomfortably, his smile fading. "Just for the duration of our journey. I told the captain that I was bringing my mate and child on board. I thought it was for the best since if someone was looking for Sultavi, they would not suspect a girl traveling with her parents. In addition, the Cire were known for their protectiveness towards their families."

Family. It was something she hadn't had in a long time, although she had done her best to create one with her students and her colleagues. Once again the tears threatened, but she forced a smile.

"I think it's an excellent idea. Now, why don't you sit down and join us? You can explain these foods," she added doubtfully, picking up a package with what looked like worms on the label. Maybe they were like gummy worms.

"Those are Herbertan mealworms," he said as he sat down, crushing her hopes. "They are very nutritious."

Even though he was on the other side of Tavi, the bench was so small that she could feel the warmth of his big body and catch his delicious, tantalizing scent. His presence was almost enough to distract her from the package of worms. Almost.

"Umm, maybe later. What else do you have?"

She ended up with some dry noodles and a sticky paste that tasted rather like dates. *At least they're a change from crackers and meat jerky*, she thought with a sigh, but she missed real food. In spite of everything, Lord K'herr had fed her well.

"I'm thirsty," Tavi announced, then made a face when Craxan handed her a container of water. "I want juice."

"We don't have juice," Joanna said gently.

"The captain does. In the galley. Right, Papa?"

"Yes." He started to stand. "Perhaps I could—"

"Sit down and finish your meal," she insisted. "Water is just fine. Isn't it, Tavi?"

The little girl nodded reluctantly, returning to her own packet of noodles with a pout, but her usual good nature had returned by the time they were finished. Joanna turned the empty packages inside out while Craxan found a marker, and Tavi settled down to draw.

A warm weight brushed against Joanna's leg and she looked down to see Craxan's tail had curved behind the little girl and reached her side. *Why did it feel so comforting?* she wondered as she ran her fingers over the intriguingly textured surface.

Craxan made that odd sound again, and she looked up to find him watching her, his eyes heated. She started to pull her hand away, but his tail curled around her fingers, then settled on her thigh.

All righty then.

Trying to ignore the oddly comforting touch, she smiled at him. "Can you tell me more about the ship?"

"What would you like to know?"

"Are there any other passengers on board?"

"I do not think so. The ship is designed to carry cargo rather than people. But it is not uncommon for this type of ship to have few small cabins that the captain can rent out in order to pick up some extra credits."

"You said a cargo ship. What is he transporting?"

"I did not ask." He gave her an apologetic look. "I suspect it is not entirely legal."

"Is that why you chose it? Because I'm not exactly legal either, am I?"

"I chose it because there would be no official record of our journey. I had not considered your status." He looked away from her, then added slowly, "Your world—does it have space flight?"

"Kind of. We've been to our moon, and some ships have reached other planets in our system. Why?"

"It is illegal to visit pre-spaceflight worlds."

"You said it was illegal to own slaves too," she said dryly. "But that didn't stop it from happening."

"The Patrol is trying to bring a halt to both activities. If... if we encounter them, they will offer to return you to your world."

Her heart skipped a beat as memories flashed through her mind. A room full of eager students. Her comfortable apartment. Her books. But then Tavi looked up at her, her little face anxious.

"You wouldn't leave me, Mama, would you?"

Her throat ached as she shook her head. "No, sweetheart. I'm not going anywhere. I would miss you too much."

"Good." Tavi nodded and returned to her drawing.

"Actually, they would wipe your memory," Craxan said softly, once Tavi was engrossed in her efforts once more.

Forget the little girl? "That would be even worse."

"I understand." He smiled at her, his eyes warm, and she believed him. Something flowed between them, a connection that should be impossible in such a short time. She found herself squeezing his tail, seeking comfort in that connection, and his eyes closed. When he opened them, his smile looked a little strained, but his voice was calm.

"Was there anything else you wanted to know about the ship?"

Oddly disappointed at the neutral question, she considered the matter. "If there aren't any other passengers, what about the crew? What size crew does it have?"

"I am not positive, but usually a ship of this size will have a crew of five or six—the captain and a navigator, a cargo master, an engineer and a mechanic, possibly a medic. Or a cook."

"A cook?" She smiled a little ruefully. "I used to enjoy cooking."

"Did you cook while you were with Lord K'herr?"

She shook her head. "Are you kidding? His head chef did not take kindly to the idea of any interference."

"He yelled at us when Mama tried to teach me," Tavi said sadly.

And went to Lord K'herr and complained. She had been told in no uncertain terms to stay out of the kitchens, and keep Sultavi out of them as well. But it gave her an idea.

"I wonder if I could get a job cooking."

"A job as a cook?" He looked so appalled she bristled.

"Why not? I may not be familiar with all the ingredients, but I can learn." Her irritation faded, replaced by anxiety. "That is, I can learn if I can find someone to teach me. Or maybe I could start out as an apprentice. But I have to find some way to support the two of us."

"That is not necessary. I will—" He came to an abrupt halt, then looked away. "Is that what Opinnas told you to do?"

"Well, no. He said he had family who would take care of us. But I don't want to be dependent on someone else, and a degree in medieval Earth history is not exactly a salable skill."

"You were a scholar?" A fleeting expression of sorrow crossed his face. "I had thought to be at one time."

"Really?" Her eyes traveled over that big, muscular body as she remembered the ease with which he had taken care of the guards. He seemed much too... physical for scholarly pursuits. *But then again, he would probably have female students fighting over his classes,* she thought crossly, then gave herself a mental shake. How ridiculous to feel jealous of imaginary females.

"What happened?"

The sorrowful expression returned, but before he could answer her, Tavi held up the drawing she had been working on so diligently.

"Look," she demanded. "I drew us."

An oversized Craxan stood next to a very round Joanna with a tiny Tavi nestled between them, while an impossibly long tail wrapped around them all. Neat but slightly lopsided letters spelled out the words, *my family*.

CHAPTER SEVEN

Craxan lifted his startled gaze from Sultavi's drawing to see Joanna looking at him, her eyes bright with unshed tears. Her hand clasped his tail so tightly that he couldn't have pulled away even if he had wanted her to release him. And he didn't. He wanted this, all of this—this female, this child, this family—so much that the ache in his chest felt like a physical wound.

But he couldn't have it, and his courage failed him.

"Please excuse me," he said, reluctantly tugging his tail away from the sweet warmth of Joanna's grip. She let him go, but her fingers caressed him as he slid free, creating shivers of pleasure despite his mental turmoil. "I need to make some... arrangements."

"But you'll be back?" Sultavi asked anxiously, while Joanna silently watched him.

"Yes, of course."

As soon as the door closed behind him, he leaned against the wall of the corridor, berating himself. *Arrangements?* A stupid excuse and far too close to a lie for his demanding conscience. But the longing that had risen inside him at the crude drawing had almost overwhelmed him.

He wanted to claim them as his own, in reality and not just as part of the job. But he had lost a family twice, and he didn't think he was strong enough to go through it again. The emptiness he had felt after Vanha's death had been deadly enough.

And even if he had been willing to take the chance, he had nothing to offer them. He'd never had a permanent home, his savings had been completely depleted in his pursuit of vengeance, and he was no longer young. His warrior skills still had value, but not on a peaceful planet like Trevelor. While he could send credits to them once he found work—and he had every intention of doing so—he would not be able to stay with them. He would not be there to make sure they were safe and well fed and happy.

Perhaps he could find another profession—although at his age and with his limited background, it seemed unlikely. As he turned over the possibilities, he remembered Joanna's suggestion that she find work as a cook. He instinctively resisted the idea that he could not provide for her, but it was a sensible suggestion and seemed important to her. Perhaps he should visit the ship's galley and see if the cook could help her learn.

As he made his way in the direction Yengik had indicated earlier, a delicious smell teased his sensitive scent receptors. The smell of roasting meat filled the corridor and he followed it to a door at the far end. He pushed it open, then ducked as a knife came flying at his head.

"I said no!" an angry voice roared.

Had he been one second slower, the knife would have penetrated his shoulder. He growled and snatched it out of the wall, then turned to look for the thrower. The only other occupant of the kitchen was a tiny, ancient Kissat, her fur white with age but her bright blue eyes glaring at him fiercely.

"Get out." Her hand reached for another knife.

"I wish to talk to you."

"I don't wish to talk to you. The last time was only a warning."

"I believe you, but this is important."

He flipped the knife in his hand, then tossed it. It landed upright in the exact center of the wooden cutting board in front of her. She looked down at the quivering handle, then back at him, then cackled loudly.

"Not bad. But now I have both knives."

He rested his hand on the hilt of the knife at his belt, and her smile broadened.

"I'm almost tempted to take you on, but lunch won't cook itself." She turned back to stir a large pot simmering over an old-fashioned burner, and he noticed for the first time that the kitchen contained a surprising array of cooking devices for a ship of this size.

"You must be Rissta." Merios's earlier amusement made sense now.

"Yeah. And you're the dumb Cire who got roped into one of my grandson's schemes."

"Grandson? Merios is your grandson?"

The swaggering captain and the ancient cook were related? Then again, perhaps it was not so far-fetched after all, he thought, as he remembered the knife throw.

"Yes. And now that I've shared our genealogy, get the hell out of my kitchen. I've got work to do."

"That is why I am here." He hesitated, not quite sure that he wanted Joanna anywhere near this fierce little female.

"Well, spit it out."

"My mate—" how easily the word came to his tongue "— enjoys cooking but she has not had much chance recently. I thought perhaps, if you were willing, she could provide you with some assistance."

"You did, did you? What kind of a male tries to put his mate to work?"

The question stung his pride. She was correct. He should be the one to provide for Joanna and Sultavi. He almost turned and walked out, but he reminded himself that this mattered to Joanna.

"One who wants to make his mate happy. This is important to her."

Rissta scowled at him, then lifted a shoulder. "I reckon I could talk to her. She's probably worthless—"

"She is not," he growled.

"—in the kitchen, but bring her along." Fierce blue eyes peered at him. "In time for the mid-shift meal. I want to watch her eat my food."

"We did not arrange to purchase meals."

She snorted. "Don't worry about it. My grandson was just being his usual annoying self. He knows that no one goes hungry when I'm cooking."

He bowed. "Thank you."

"Don't think you're going to impress me with those fancy-ass Cire manners," she sniffed, and waved her spoon at him. "Now get out."

"Yes, ma'am."

Fighting the urge to return to the cabin immediately, he went to the exercise room instead, determined to bring himself under control. An hour later, he was dripping with sweat and his body ached, but as soon as he opened the door to the cabin and the two females smiled up at him, a wave of longing almost took him to his knees.

"I must shower," he said desperately and stumbled into the small facility. He set the cleansing liquid to icy cold and took a few deep calming breaths, but Joanna's scent lingered here, and his body responded. He achieved nothing but a cold, aching cock. And a wet uniform.

He started to strip it off, then remembered that his clothing was in the outer cabin. With a sigh, he cracked open the door panel. "Could you hand me my pack, please?"

"What pack?" Joanna asked.

The intriguing pink washed over her cheeks as she surveyed his naked chest, and her scent increased. His body pleased her? Making sure to stay out of Sultavi's line of sight, he opened the door a little more, enough that she could see his wet pants clinging to the thick ridge of his shaft. Her plump little lips parted, and he remembered how delightful they had felt against his cheek.

His cock stiffened even more, the broad head threatening to push up past the waistband of his pants, and her eyes widened. He had the sudden impulse to pull it free, to show her how much she affected him, but then he heard the rustle of paper and he yanked the waistband higher, ignoring the painful constriction.

Fuck. He was supposed to be bringing himself under control, not succumbing to temptation.

"My pack," he repeated, his voice hoarse.

The rosy glow covered her entire face now as she hastily snatched her gaze away. "Where is it?"

"The second compartment above the table on the left."

She nodded and moved out of sight, returning a second later with the worn black pack. "Here."

As she thrust it at him, their fingers touched and it was all he could do not to pull her against him. "Thank you."

"You're welcome," she whispered, but she didn't move away.

"I, umm, need to dress."

"Then your tail had better release me."

He looked down to find his tail lodged securely around the tantalizing softness of her waist. At least he hadn't pulled her closer the way he had considered. With a sigh, he forced his tail to let go. She hesitated for a fraction of a second, then stepped back.

When he emerged in a dry uniform, she was looking at another of Sultavi's drawings, but her cheeks were still pink.

"I talked to the cook," he said. "She might be willing to let you assist her."

"Really?" Her eyes lit up. "That would be wonderful."

"I am not sure you will consider it so wonderful after you meet her."

"Why? What's she like?"

"I think I will let you decide for yourself. She has invited us to join her for the mid-shift meal."

"Does that mean I can have juice?" Sultavi asked hopefully.

He laughed. "You will have to ask her."

They both stood, and he folded away the table. After a brief hesitation, he handed Joanna her cloak. He hadn't seen any other males but Yengik and the captain—and he hoped they would not encounter them—but he would feel better if she was covered.

She silently wrapped it around her shoulders, then startled him by reaching out and touching his arm. Her pale fingers looked tiny against the muscles of his forearm, but they looked so right.

"Thank you for arranging this, Craxan."

"It seemed important to you."

"It is." She squeezed his arm, then let him go. He wanted to demand that she put her hand back in its rightful place, but she had already turned to the child.

"Are you ready, Tavi?"

"Yes!"

He paused at the door long enough to add Joanna's retinal scan to the lock, then led them out into the corridor. Sultavi took off running, her purple locks glinting in the artificial light.

"Yengik said it was this way," she called.

Joanna laughed. "I think she's excited. But you said she was safe, right?"

"I believe so." *But better to be sure.* "Wait at the end of the corridor, Tavi."

The little girl obeyed, spinning in circles and giggling as she waited for him, for *them*. His chest started to ache again, but he no longer wanted to push it away. For right now, they were his and he would soak in every minute, no matter how painful it would be in the end.

When they reached the galley, he knocked, not about to take the chance of a knife flying towards one of his females.

"Come," Rissta ordered brusquely.

Sultavi's eyes widened as they stepped into the galley and saw the old female with her knife waiting for them. A tiny hand crept into his, and he curled his tail around her shoulders.

"Rissta, this is my mate, Joanna, and my daughter, Sultavi." How right the words sounded.

"So you think you can assist me, human?"

He flashed Rissta a startled look. How had she known that Joanna was human? But her eyes were on Joanna and not on him.

"I hope so. I used to cook a lot."

"Professionally?"

"No. For my friends and my students."

He could hear the slight strain in Joanna's voice, and he put a comforting hand on her back. Perhaps this wasn't the best idea...

"Do you have juice?" Sultavi asked.

The intense stare switched to his daughter, and he thought the old female's face softened.

"I might. Have you been a good girl?"

"Very good. Right, Papa?"

"Yes, princess."

Rissta sniffed. "Shame. Sometimes you need to be bad. But I reckon I can find you something."

Nerves forgotten, the girl bounced happily over to the table. Joanna gave him a confused look and followed.

"Well, take off that cloak, human. You're not going to get cold if you're working."

"My name is Joanna." There was an edge to his female's voice as she slipped off the cloak and revealed her outfit.

"White?" Rissta snorted. "Not very practical in a kitchen."

"It's all I have," Joanna said, lifting her chin. Her quiet dignity impressed him, even as he berated himself for not having thought to provide her with additional clothing. Even if this was only temporary, he should be doing a better job of caring for his females.

"Hmph." The sharp blue eyes surveyed his female. "You couldn't wear anything of mine, but there's some fabric in the stores. You could make something."

"I'm afraid I don't really know how to sew."

"I do," he volunteered, and all three females looked at him with the same shocked expression. "I cannot make anything elaborate, but I should be able to make a simple gown."

"Me too, Papa," Sultavi begged. "I miss my pretty clothes."

Rissta looked at the little girl, then back at him, but to his vast relief, she didn't pursue the subject.

"Go see Anaeus," she ordered. "He's the cargo master. Tell him I said to let you choose some fabric."

He hesitated, and Rissta waved her hand impatiently. "Go on now. These two are safe with me."

"Do I have your word?"

Rissta gave him a disgusted look, then deliberately placed her hand on one of her knives. "No harm will come to them."

"We're fine," Joanna assured him, and even Sultavi nodded.

Oddly disgruntled that he was no longer needed, he left the galley and headed for the store room.

He disliked the cargo master on sight. An overweight Persat male in elaborate finery—completely out of place on a ship like this—he smirked at Craxan.

"So you're the captain's pet Cire."

"I am the pet of no one," he growled, but Anaeus only laughed.

"Of course not. What would you like? I have a wide variety of supplies, although most of them are quite expensive." He ran a disparaging eye over Craxan's worn uniform.

"Rissta said to let me choose some fabric for my females."

As soon as he said the words, he knew he had made a mistake. Anaeus's eyes lit up with a speculative gleam.

"Did you say females? How many do you have?"

"Two. My mate and my child."

"And you intend to keep both of them? They are quite val—"

His words cut off with a muffled gurgle as Craxan grabbed him by the neck and hauled him up against the wall.

"They are not possessions to be bartered. You will never refer to them in those terms again."

Anaeus made a strangled noise, and Craxan dropped him with a disgusted grunt.

"I meant no harm," the other male rasped. Despite his apologetic words, his eyes brimmed with anger.

"Where is the cloth?"

"The smaller lengths are along the far wall."

He turned in that direction without bothering to respond. The selection was somewhat limited, but he chose a practical dark blue fabric, then impulsively threw in a length of deep gold that would bring out the golden highlights in Joanna's hair and a small piece in shimmering white for Sultavi.

Anaeus measured them out without a word, then handed him a datapad to sign.

"I'll leave the captain to sort out the reckoning," he muttered.

"Very well."

He took the fabric and left without another word, making a mental note to tell Joanna to stay well clear of the other male. Something about him made his skin twitch, and he had been a soldier for long enough not to ignore his intuition.

But in the meantime, he had clothing to prepare for his females.

CHAPTER EIGHT

Joanna took a deep breath after Craxan left, then smiled tentatively at the tiny alien female with the sharp knives. She had almost feline features, with two small horns poking through a curly white mane. The rest of her fur was white as well, and Joanna wondered if it was her natural coloring or due to her age.

"Thank you for offering to help me learn," she said sincerely.

"We'll see." Rissta sniffed. "Sit down."

The table in the center of the room might be metal, but it reminded her of her own kitchen table and she felt surprisingly comfortable as she watched the other female bustle around.

Rissta handed Sultavi a glass of pale green juice, then gave one to Joanna. She watched expectantly as Joanna took a sip.

"This is laimi juice, isn't it? But you've added something."

"Farlan salt. Brings out the flavor," Rissta said. "Next test."

That had been a test? Joanna gulped. "I'm only familiar with the food we ate on Alliko."

"The principles don't change. Here. What do you think of this?"

The small purple cracker was shockingly bitter, but she did her best not to reveal her dislike. She must not have been entirely successful because Rissta barked a laugh, then handed her another plate.

"Which of these three cheeses would you pair with it?"

As soon as she tried the second one, she knew it was perfect. The cheese had a slight underlying sweetness which offset the bitterness so that the two complemented each other.

"This one."

"Hmph. You may have enough of a palette to be worth teaching. But eat first."

Rissta gave them both steaming bowls of soup and thick slices of bread. The soup was an unappetizing grey, and even though Sultavi dove in happily, Joanna only took a cautious sip. The flavor exploded in her mouth, rich and meaty with a slight peppery undertone.

"This is amazing. What is it?"

"Herbertan mealworms, seasoned with spice."

Joanna almost choked, but she forced herself to smile. "It's delicious."

Rissta's sharp eyes apparently didn't miss anything. "Yes it is, and if you're squeamish, you'd better get over it now."

The implication was clear, and she took another spoonful. It really was delicious and after all, there were plenty of things on Earth that seemed unlikely sources of food. Like oysters.

Rissta gave an approving grunt as she took the empty bowl. "I'm willing to give you a try. Let's see if you can follow orders."

For the rest of the afternoon, she chopped—and re-chopped when Rissta wasn't satisfied with the precision of the pieces—and stirred and tasted and listened as Rissta lectured. Even though there was an overwhelming amount to learn, she had been correct about one thing. She knew she could do this.

"Thank you," she said sincerely when Rissta finally declared that everything was ready for the evening meal. The other female had already informed her that they would not be dining with the crew, which suited her perfectly.

Rissta peered at her, then gave a reluctant sniff. "You did well enough. For a human."

She had said something similar when they first met, and it suddenly occurred to Joanna to wonder how Rissta had known she was human. But before she could ask, Sultavi interrupted them, holding up a lopsided tart. The little girl had spent most of the afternoon playing with pieces of dough, rolling them out and cutting them into shapes, then gleefully mashing them back into a ball.

"Look!"

"That looks delicious, Tavi. Are you going to eat it now?"

"No, I want to take it back to Papa."

An unexpected lump rose in her throat as she added the tart to the collection of dishes Rissta insisted they take with them. Acting the part of a family was becoming a little too real —and too tempting. This was a job for Craxan, nothing more, and they would be parting ways soon. She needed to put some distance between them.

A resolve that disappeared as soon as they entered the cabin and found Craxan surrounded by pieces of fabric, a distraught look on his face. Apparently he had somewhat overstated his sewing skills in his anxiousness to provide clothes for them. Her heart melted.

"Where's my dress?" Sultavi asked as soon as they entered.

"I am not that fast, princess, and I will need to take some measurements." He gave Joanna a rueful smile. "I am afraid my skills are somewhat rusty. But in the meantime, I brought you some of my clothing. I believe black will be more practical than your current outfit."

He ran his eyes over her as she discarded her cloak. The white silk had taken some damage, but she suspected that he wasn't looking for stains. Her nipples beaded at the warmth in his eyes.

She tried to laugh, but it came out breathlessly. "You're right. And it will be nice to have a change."

"Me too," Sultavi demanded.

"Of course." He held up a sleeveless black shirt. "This is one of my training shirts. I can cut it to fit you, then use it as a pattern."

With Joanna's help, he managed to take Sultavi's measurements. He cut the cloth with an unexpectedly sure hand, then used a heated tool to close the seams. Her daughter pranced around excitedly in the resulting dress.

"I look like Papa," she said happily, smoothing down the black cloth.

"You did a good job," Joanna told Craxan.

He shook his head. "The right seam is crooked, and the hemline—"

She put her fingers over his lips and he froze. "You did a good job. She's very happy."

His mouth parted, and for the briefest instant she felt his tongue touch her fingers before he curled his hand around hers and placed it on his chest. Did even his tongue have those same intriguing nubs? The thought sent a spark of excitement straight to her clit, but she forced herself to ignore it and concentrate on his words.

"I am happy that she is satisfied. It has been a long time, and I am out of practice."

"How did you learn?"

"Necessity." He was still holding her hand and he played

with it as he spoke. "When Vanha and I left Ciresia, we had no money and very few possessions. It took time to find jobs. To gain a reputation. So I did everything I could to make the credits stretch. It was not that much of a leap from repairing a weapons harness to repairing clothing and eventually creating it."

He sounded nostalgic, and she wanted to ask him more, but Sultavi interrupted.

"When are we going to eat? I'm hungry."

She saw the distress on Craxan's face and squeezed his hand. "She's not that hungry. Miss Rissta was feeding her tidbits all afternoon."

Tavi gave her an innocent look. "She just gave me a few bites. And I want to give Papa his surprise."

Craxan still looked worried so she gave in. "All right. Let's put this fabric away, and then we can eat."

He obeyed, folding the fabric and putting it in yet another wall compartment. She caught the flash of gold and wondered what else he had stored there, but then Tavi almost spilled the soup in her eagerness to help and she went to her aid.

The meal was a success. The bench was too small, and Tavi knocked over her precious bottle of juice, but it didn't matter. The food was delicious, but it was more than that. She told Craxan about her afternoon, and he shared some humorous stories of his own cooking attempts, while Tavi provided her own commentary. It felt like the type of warm, family meal that she had always longed to have, and she stopped trying to remember that it was just temporary and enjoyed herself.

Craxan was lavish in his praise of everything, especially Tavi's tart. The little girl watched anxiously as he took a careful bite and chewed thoughtfully.

"I believe this is the best tart I have ever eaten," he said finally.

Tavi grinned and threw herself at him. "I made it especially for you."

"Thank you, princess. It was perfect."

An unexpected lump sprang to her throat as she watched the small head tucked so trustingly against that broad chest. Then his tail touched her wrist and she looked up to find him watching her. There was a question in his eyes, but she couldn't bring herself to acknowledge it. Instead, she jumped to her feet and started stacking the dishes.

"Craxan, can you return these to the galley while I give Tavi a bath—I mean, a shower. Tell Rissta I will clean them tomorrow."

"Of course I will return them. And wash them," he said immediately.

"You don't need to do that."

"You prepared the meal. I will clean."

"It was mainly Rissta."

"I will clean," he repeated, gathered up the dishes, and left.

"Is he coming back, Mama?" Tavi asked.

"Of course sweetheart," she said, realizing that she had absolutely no doubt that he would. "Now let's get you ready for bed."

A clean Sultavi insisted on putting on her new black outfit, and Joanna couldn't blame her. She gave her own clothes a rueful look. In addition to the side effects of her kitchen work, she was now damp from wrestling with Tavi and she could see the shadow of her areola beneath her top.

An effect that Craxan noticed immediately upon his return. He froze in the doorway, his eyes going directly to her breasts, and her nipples responded, thrusting against the cool, damp cloth. She crossed her arms over her breasts and did her best to ignore the low ache between her thighs.

"I was wondering if I could also borrow one of your shirts."

"I have not yet had a chance to measure you." His voice deepened as he took a step closer and she could all too clearly imagine his big hands running down her sides, cupping her breasts...

"I have a better idea," she said quickly. "I can just wear it as is tonight and then tomorrow you can use this top as a pattern."

"Very well," he agreed, but as he went to retrieve his pack, he bent down and whispered in her ear. "But my way would be far more interesting."

Her cheeks flamed as she grabbed the shirt he handed her and ducked into the bathroom. He followed her in, his body pressing against hers as he leaned over and touched the wall. A small panel slid aside, revealing another compartment.

"To keep your clothes dry," he explained. "Although I am not sure I regret not informing you of that previously."

He left before she could think of a response.

As she stripped off her clothes and placed them in the compartment, her body still hummed with excitement from being pressed against him. From the massive bar of flesh that had been pressed against her ass, he had been just as excited. His scent lingered, even after she turned on the shower liquid, both comforting and arousing. She found herself cupping her breasts, sliding her soapy hands over them as she imagined that Craxan was the one touching her. She pinched her nipples, a little harder than she intended, but the resulting sting sent a streak of excitement straight to her clit.

With a guilty look at the closed door, she slid her hand between her legs. The little nub of flesh was already swollen, hot to her touch, and she circled it slowly, imagining one of those big fingers caressing her, sliding deeper, preparing her for his cock... She came with a gasp, a warm tide of pleasure rolling over her.

How long *had* it been? She certainly hadn't thought about

sex during the year of her captivity, and even back on Earth, she hadn't been that interested since she and Gary separated. *Or even before we parted ways,* she thought dryly as she resumed washing. But a few heated looks from a big, green alien, and her sex drive came roaring back.

It's just because we're in such close proximity, she told herself firmly. But when she walked out of the bathroom dressed in his oversized shirt and saw him watching her, his eyes warm, her heart skipped a beat.

"Tell me a story, Mama," Sultavi demanded. "Papa doesn't know the same ones."

"Probably not." She sat down on the bench and lifted her daughter onto her lap. "Can you dim the lights, Craxan?"

He obeyed and she gathered Tavi close, telling her an old favorite. Craxan's tail wrapped around them both, just like in Tavi's picture, and she felt surprisingly content. She didn't know what the future held, but tonight, she was happy.

When Sultavi fell asleep, Craxan lifted her into the upper bunk, and then they sat talking in the dim light. The shadowy space felt warm and intimate, and she was overwhelmingly conscious of his closeness. His tail was back on her leg and it would be all too easy to slide over just a little bit more and...

"How long has it been since you were taken?" he asked, distracting her wayward thoughts.

"An Earth year. Three hundred and sixty-five days, more or less. I may have lost count at the beginning."

"Do you miss it?"

"Sometimes. I had a very nice life. A job I loved, an apartment on the edge of campus filled with books and plants." She ran her fingers thoughtfully over his tail. "But I've been here so long. Sometimes it feels as if that life was only a dream."

His face looked oddly strained. "What about friends, family? A mate?"

"I had friends, of course. We weren't one of those high-pressure universities, and I got along with my colleagues. No relatives. I was a late—and I think unexpected—addition to my parents' marriage. They were both gone before I was taken. What about you?"

"There is no one."

The words sounded so harsh, so lonely. She patted his tail soothingly, waiting to see if he would add anything more.

"I had a big family once," he said finally. "Two brothers, a sister, lots of cousins. The plague took every one of them."

She couldn't imagine how terrible that must have been. The loss of her parents had devastated her, but she had only lost two people.

"How old were you?"

"I had just turned eighteen. The government was telling everyone that it was our duty to try and restore our society. I... could not. Vanha had been one of my teachers at the academy. He was the one who got me away from Ciresia. Because of him, I learned that my skills had value."

She didn't respond, but her face must have given her away because a faint smile twisted his mouth.

"I suppose it doesn't look like that now. It's been a bad year."

"Why?"

"Vanha died six months ago. Died stupidly. Took some money from the wrong people, then drank too much, and let himself be cornered. He still managed to take out three of them, but the other two killed him."

His tail had turned rigid beneath her fingers.

"I should have been there," he burst out. "But we had argued earlier that year and I was still sulking."

"I'm so sorry."

"I spent the past six months, and what was left of my savings, hunting down the two that got away."

"Did you find them?"

"Yes. And I avenged him. But after that... there just did not seem to be much point to my life. I was not in a good place when Jed brought me the message from Opinnas."

"But you came. And you saved us."

"Or perhaps you saved me."

They looked at each other and she could feel the tension between them, like a glowing ember that needed only the slightest spark to make it flare.

"You said you had no children," he said slowly.

"No. At first I was concentrating on getting my doctorate. And then I was in a... relationship for a long time with another professor."

"A mate?" he growled.

"No, neither one of us was interested in getting married. We didn't even live together, but we did spend a lot of time together. It was... comfortable. He wasn't interested in children, and I suppose I didn't really think about it. Then when we finally broke up—"

"He broke you?" His expression was horrified.

She laughed. "Not at all. It's just an expression that means we stopped being together. He took a position at another university, and I decided not to go with him. We parted on good terms. I even went to his wedding." *Less than a year later.* Apparently he had been interested in marriage after all—just not with her. "At that point, I decided I was too old and set in my ways to have kids. It didn't really bother me."

Or at least that's what I always told myself.

"But then Lord K'herr brought me to Sultavi, and now I know what it's like to have a daughter. I will never give her up."

Her chest ached at the thought of being separated from her daughter, but the future seemed so tenuous.

"How long will it take to get to Trevelor?" she asked, trying to distract herself before she panicked.

"A little over a week."

"I didn't think it was that far."

"Captain Merios is making a detour to Driguera to pick up some cargo." His face hardened. "It is my job to provide security for him there."

Security? Her throat tightened. "Will that be dangerous?"

He shrugged a massive shoulder. "The place does not have a good reputation, but I can handle myself. That is why the captain was willing to exchange my services for this cabin."

He had done so much for them already, and now he was going to be putting himself at greater risk. Overcome with gratitude, she leaned up and kissed his cheek. When she pulled back, his hand came up to cover the place her lips had touched. Had she offended him?

"You did that before. When we arrived."

Her cheeks warmed. "I did. It's called a kiss. Is that something your people do?"

"No."

"Oh. I'm sorry if it bothers you."

"It does not bother me." That disturbing heat was back in his eyes. "As I said, my people do not perform the act, but I have seen it done."

"Just seen it?"

He inclined his head, then said softly. "A Cire male only finds true satisfaction with his mate. Only then will his cock knot inside her and provide release."

A sudden rush of heat filled her as she imagined that already huge cock expanding inside her. But then she thought about the implications of his words.

"Does that mean you've never..."

"When Vanha and I first left Ciresia, I was young and rebellious. I... tried the act a few times, but it was unsatisfactory. The females did not feel right, did not smell right, and I was more alone afterwards. I should have waited."

His tail stroked her bare leg, the end slipping towards her inner thigh, as his hand came up to play with her hair.

"Every part of you is soft. Your skin. Your hair. Your mouth."

His eyes focused on her mouth, and she licked suddenly dry lips. Her nipples tightened into aching little points, and she could feel a throbbing ache low in her stomach. His nostrils flared.

"You have the most amazing scent. So sweet and tempting. Would you taste as sweet, I wonder."

That same reckless urge took over. She rose up on her knees and took his face in her hands. "Why don't you decide for yourself?"

She pressed her lips against the thin line of his lips. He didn't respond at first, but then he said he'd only seen someone kiss. She licked the seam of his mouth, lightly, teasingly, until he groaned and his lips parted. Her tongue darted inside, and lord, he tasted amazing. His tongue touched hers tentatively, and she felt the small nubs that covered it just before he groaned again and took control. His hand came up to hold her head in place as he plundered her mouth, exploring every part. His other hand dropped down to her ass as he yanked her against him, reaching beneath the shirt to squeeze the soft flesh.

It wasn't until she felt his tail sliding between her legs that she came to her senses and tried to draw back. He released her immediately, but his tail remained wrapped around her waist as they stared at each other.

"I—"

"Don't you dare say you're sorry," she said fiercely. "I was the one who kissed you."

His hand went to his mouth. "And now I understand why people kiss." He reached over and traced his thumb along her lower lip. "Your lips are swollen."

She licked them deliberately, catching his thumb. "Good. They should be after a kiss like that."

"You are satisfied?"

Satisfied? When her breasts felt swollen and achy and her clit throbbed?

"No," she said quietly. "But I enjoyed our kiss very much."

"As did I. Perhaps we could do it again?"

It would undoubtedly be a mistake. After he took them to Trevelor, she would probably never see him again and that knowledge already made her chest ache. But they were together now, and she felt reckless and sensual and alive in a way she hadn't felt for a very long time.

"Yes," she whispered, and reached for him.

CHAPTER NINE

Craxan stared into the darkness, his arms and tail wrapped snugly around the female in his arms.

His female.

His *mate*.

He had been sure of it before, but after last night there was no doubt. His arms tightened around her sleeping figure, his head filled with her scent. Her peaceful breaths feathered across his bare chest, an exquisite torture to his aching cock. At some point during their kissing session, she had insisted that he remove his shirt, running her hands greedily over his bare skin and pressing hot little kisses to the exposed flesh.

He had dared to suggest that she do the same, but she cast a meaningful glance at the overhead bunk and refused. She had permitted him to slip his hands beneath her shirt, to feel the lush fullness of her breasts filling his palms and the hard little points of her nipples between his fingers. He longed to see them, to taste them, and when she arched into his touch and the scent of her arousal filled the cabin, a previously unknown primitive instinct urged him to rip away the shirt and claim her completely.

But she trusted him, and there was a child sleeping nearby, and he called on all of the discipline he had learned over the years to restrain himself. A discipline that had been no help at all when it came to his unruly tail. She had told him that they could only go to second base, a strange expression which meant he could not touch her below the waist. But as their kisses grew hotter and he explored her luscious breasts and she panted into his mouth, his tail had slipped between her legs and found a hot, wet nub of flesh that quivered at his touch. His tail tugged at it lightly, and she jerked in his arms, burying her face against his neck to hide her muffled cry.

He felt her shudder, felt a rush of liquid heat bathing his tail, and was reaching to free his erection before he came to his senses. He could not.

Losing her would devastate him now, but if he entered her, if he knotted inside her... He would never recover.

Instead, he regretfully pulled his tail free. He could not resist tasting her passion, and the delicious essence almost overrode his good sense once again. But then she looked up at him, her eyes dazed, and smiled.

"I think you broke the rules."

"I did not touch you with my hands."

She shook her head, but she was still smiling. "I don't believe I restricted it to hands. If I used my mouth on you, that would definitely be going beyond second base."

"Your mouth?"

"To... kiss you. Here."

For one delightful second, her fingers traced the ridge of his erection. He almost exploded, not just from her touch but from the shockingly erotic thought of her mouth on his cock. The act had been banned on Cire as soon as the Council realized how few females were left. The only purpose for a male's seed was for procreation. Since then he had seen enough to realize that it was a common act, but enough of his upbringing remained that it had the thrill of the forbidden.

"I... I..." He could not find the words, but she pulled him back down and there was no more need to talk.

He wasn't sure how long they had spent kissing and touching, but he was quite sure that he had brought her to climax twice more before she drifted off into an exhausted sleep. He had not. Instead he had held her and listened to her breathe and tried to come up with a way for them to be together. He was searching for a planet that would be safe enough for his females but still provide him with work when he heard a quiet whisper.

"Papa?"

"Yes, Tavi?"

"Is it time to get up yet?"

By the ship's settings, it was early morning. "I suppose so."

"Is Mama still asleep?" Her little voice sounded distinctly disapproving.

"Yes, she was very tired." *At least in part due to my efforts,* he thought, feeling both proud and a little guilty. "What if we go and see if Miss Risstã is awake?"

"You had better leave Mama a note this time," she giggled.

"I will," he promised, turning up the cabin lights just enough that he could see.

He pulled on his shirt, wrote the note, and lifted Sultavi down from her bunk. She yawned and snuggled against him as his tail curved protectively around her small figure. There had to be a way, he decided. He would not let them out of his life.

"You do not seem very awake," he said.

"I just need juice."

He laughed and carried her out of the cabin.

Rissta was awake. She grunted at the sight of them, but supplied Sultavi with juice and biscuits. She even unbent enough to hand him a cup of hot tea and a plate of fried ova.

"Thank you. This is delicious."

"Hmph." Despite the grunt, she seemed pleased at his praise and joined them at the table with her own cup of tea. "Your mate did not do badly yesterday. But why is this so important to her?"

"She thinks she could get a job as a cook," he admitted.

"Why would she need to?"

"A mercenary's pay can be... uncertain."

"And if you're off looking for work and she's cooking, who's going to take care of this one?" Rissta jerked her thumb at Sultavi.

She didn't wait for a response, changing the subject to the shortcomings of her grandson. He couldn't help but smile at her bitingly accurate portrayal of Merios, but her words haunted him. He hated the idea of Joanna struggling to cope with a job and a child with no help.

As if thinking of her had conjured her up, Joanna appeared at the entrance to the kitchen. She still looked sleepy and tousled and absolutely adorable, especially when her cheeks turned pink as she gave him a shy glance. He wanted to pick her up and carry her back to bed—and his cock vehemently agreed—but she was already moving into the room and greeting Rissta and Sultavi.

When she came to him, his tail curved around her waist and tucked her firmly against his side. When she didn't object, he followed up by brushing his mouth to hers.

"Good morning, my mate."

"Good morning. Thank you for leaving me the note, but you should have woken me."

"You were sleeping so peacefully that I did not want to

disturb you. You had a late night."

She blushed again and he gave her a quick hug, then looked up to see Tavi giggling at them and Rissta staring thoughtfully.

"Go on, boy," the old female said brusquely. "I'm sure you have something better to do with your time than clutter up my kitchen."

He didn't, but he gave in to the inevitable. After another kiss for his mate and a hug from Tavi, he left the kitchen and went to the exercise room. Jed was already there, looking tired.

"Is something wrong?"

"No more than usual." The male rubbed his thumb over his fingers, a habit Craxan had noted before. "A long flight gives you too much time to think. To remember."

He knew those long, empty nights all too well, but since he had met Joanna and Sultavi, his thoughts had been full of them.

"Perhaps you should find a mate," he suggested.

Jed shot him a discerningly sharp look. "Why do I suspect that this is no longer just a job?"

"Because it is not."

"I am happy for you, even if it means the end of our brief association."

He sighed heavily as he stripped down to a pair of training shorts. "I am not sure that it will be. They are planning to stay on Trevelor. There is not exactly a high demand for my skills on a peaceful planet like that."

Jed nodded. "I would have the same problem—my expertise is in ship engines. Not that I will ever have a mate."

"Why not?"

"After what I did? I don't deserve one." He was rubbing his thumb again. "And what if I can't continue to control the drinking?"

Craxan wished he had an easy answer, but he had seen enough to know that it was a difficult struggle.

"Perhaps a mate could help with that," he suggested.

Jed looked shocked. "But it would be my duty to care for her."

"I suspect my mate would say that each of you should care for the other."

The subject made him uncomfortable, especially since he was so conscious of his own shortcomings in his ability to care for his mate and child.

"Let us train," he said, changing the subject. "Perhaps I can show you some additional tactics—so you will not be bested in three moves."

Jed grinned fiercely. "You're on."

By the end of the training session, Craxan was exhausted and he could feel a bone deep bruise on his left shoulder where Jed had managed to land a blow, but he was also filled with satisfaction. Jed had done well in response to his tutelage. He dropped down against one wall, and Jed joined him, passing him a bottle of water.

"Thank you," the other male said. "That was very helpful."

Craxan shrugged, but he appreciated the other male's thanks. "You have a good foundation. You just need to strengthen your stance and learn to use your opponent's strength against them."

They drank the water in silence for a few moments, then Jed said hesitantly. "Have you considered becoming an instructor? Not only do you have the skills, but you're also able to share that knowledge."

His lips twisted. "I had intended to be a teacher once—a scholar. That is not exactly what I had in mind."

"You should consider it. I suspect there is a need for that—even on a planet like Trevelor. Maybe even more so since they are not natural warriors." Jed stood and offered a hand to Craxan. "It's time for my shift. But think about it."

Craxan rose, thinking about the other male's words as he toweled off. It was true that he was well trained. While most of his jobs were solitary, he had occasionally worked with younger males and showed them additional techniques. The job would not be glamorous, nor would it pay as well as his current occupation, but as long as it paid enough to provide Joanna and Tavi with decent food and adequate shelter, he would be satisfied.

The idea continued to turn in his brain over the next few days, but he could not bring himself to mention it to Joanna. Instead he allowed himself to fall into the comfortable rhythm of life on board. Joanna spent at least half of each day in the kitchens with Rissta and he used that time to sew or to train or to entertain Tavi. They spent the rest of the day together—as a family.

And the nights. At night, she was all his. They would talk and she would tell him of her previous life and sometimes she coaxed part of his history from him.

But even when they were just talking casually, her presence made his blood hum and his cock stiffen, and at some point, she would come into his arms. After the second time his tail brought her to climax, she had abandoned her second base rule. She had been lying back in his arms, her face still flushed and her eyes heavy, and smiled up at him.

"I suppose I should just admit that we have reached third base."

"Is there a fourth? Or perhaps a fifth?" His mind reeled at the possibilities.

"Only a fourth." The color deepened on her cheeks, but she did not look away from him. "That would be intercourse."

His cock jerked so hard that he was afraid his pants would split open. He was beginning to think that his erection would never fade, and although he had tried taking himself in hand during his showers, it had been meaningless and unsatisfactory.

He wanted to bury himself inside her more than he had ever wanted anything in his entire life, but he would not take that step until he could claim her as his mate.

"But there are many other steps between these bases of yours." He ran his tail lightly over her clit as he spoke.

"Many other steps?" she asked teasingly.

Emboldened by her provocative smile, he slid his hand between her legs and thrust a thick finger into her small channel. She was still slick and hot from her climax, but her sweet little cunt clung to him. She gasped, but she didn't pull away and when his tail circled her swollen pearl again, he felt her quiver around his finger.

"Perhaps this is base three point one," he suggested, beginning to thrust slowly in and out of her.

"Y-Yes," she stuttered. "We shouldn't forget three point one."

Her hips were arching up to meet his strokes, and he offered her his other hand. They had discovered that she had a tendency to cry out when she climaxed, and she liked to hold his hand over her mouth to muffle the sound.

Since then they had discovered other steps on the path between bases—three point two and three point four were his personal favorites—but he had so far refused to let her touch him in the same way. He suspected that one touch of her hand or her mouth on his cock and his few remaining shreds of control would vanish. He would claim her, and she would be his forever.

But he had not taken that step. He told himself it was because of the uncertain future, but deep down, he knew it was more. He had not realized until he lost Vanha how much that sense of family meant to him. The loss of it had almost destroyed him, and he was afraid.

Then, on the afternoon of the fourth day, he went to the

kitchen to collect Joanna and Tavi and found Rissta scowling at his mate.

"What is happening?" he asked.

"Miss Rissta says we have to eat with the crew," Sultavi said happily. "I think it will be fun to have dinner with Yengik. Maybe the captain will magic some more sweets."

He looked over to see Joanna giving him a worried frown.

"I really don't think that's a good idea—" she said, but Rissta interrupted.

"If you are cooking for others, you need to see how they respond to your food." The elderly female scowled. "If you are not prepared to do that, then I have nothing else to teach you."

"But..." Joanna gave him a helpless look.

He understood her hesitation. He had been equally reluctant to expose his two females to the rest of the small crew. Even Jed had not actually met them. Perhaps he was being foolish. What harm could come to them here under his protection?

"I am sure it will be fine," he assured her.

Sultavi cheered and Rissta cackled. "New mates are always so protective. You'll get over it soon enough, boy."

He somehow doubted that, but he merely bowed his head and escorted his family back to the cabin.

"I want to wear the pink—" Tavi began, then her little face fell. "I forgot I don't have my pretty dresses anymore. Father always liked me to wear one at dinner."

She rarely mentioned her biological parent, and he immediately wanted to comfort her. He had intended to keep it a surprise for when they landed on Trevelor, but after a look at that woebegone little face, he went to the compartment where he kept his sewing supplies and pulled out the dress he had made her from the white silk.

"It is not pink, but perhaps you would like to wear this?" he asked gently.

"Oh, Papa." She ran a tentative finger along the shimmering fabric. "It's so pretty."

"Not as pretty as you are."

She giggled, then flung her arms around his neck. "I love it. Thank you."

"Perhaps you should try it on first," he warned her. With practice he had remembered more of those long-ago days and his skills had improved, but he was far from being a tailor.

"I love it," she said firmly. "Look, Mama."

"Very pretty." Joanna smiled at her. "You will be the belle of the ball."

"Like in the story? Does that mean there's a beast?"

"Only Papa when he growls."

Tavi giggled, and his mate arched an eyebrow at him. She knew full well the best way to make him growl. He hesitated for a moment, then retrieved the second gown.

"This one is for you."

"For me? You shouldn't have done that."

"Of course I should. You should always be clothed in the finest manner—not that this is the finest, but it is the best I can do. I wish I could provide you with more," he said regretfully.

"Don't be silly." She gave him a teasing look. "This would be completely impractical in the kitchen. Rissta would never let me hear the end of it."

Her words did not ease his consciousness of his failings. "You should not have to work in the kitchen."

She reached over and put her hand on his arm. "I love working in the kitchen, and I love—love that you made it possible."

He couldn't doubt her sincerity, and he sighed and pulled her close.

CHAPTER TEN

Craxan left the cabin so they could dress, and Joanna found herself staring at the door as it closed behind him. She had come so close to telling him she loved him. But she was scared. Not so much of her own feelings—despite the short time they had been together, she felt closer to him than she had ever felt to another man—but whether he felt the same way.

As easily as he had slipped into the role of mate, and father, he had never said that it was more than a job to him. He had never mentioned a future together. And yes, he was sweet and kind and wonderful, but maybe that was just his nature.

"Help me, Mama," Tavi demanded, drawing her out of her speculations. She had one arm trapped in the armhole of the black dress Craxan had made for her.

Joanna laughed and went to her assistance.

The white dress looked wonderful on Tavi. The fabric had a faint, iridescent shimmer that brought out the lavender undertones in her daughter's skin and contrasted beautifully with her deep purple hair. At Tavi's request, she even braided some of her hair to reveal her small horns. She could almost have been going off to one of Lord K'herr's formal events, and for a moment guilt gripped her.

She had taken Sultavi away from everything—away from a beautiful home and a promising future and a significant fortune. *And away from the monster T'paja who only wants to use her*, she reminded herself. She might not be able to provide her daughter with material wealth, but she could give her unlimited love.

"Now you," Tavi said, twirling around to watch her skirt flare out.

Joanna picked up her own dress. Craxan had already made her two sets of pants and tunics modeled after her nightwear. They were practical and surprisingly comfortable, but they were far from glamorous. *But this dress is the epitome of glamor*, she thought as she ran her fingers over the shimmering gold fabric that reminded her of heavy satin.

The silky cloth even smelled wonderful, and it took her a moment to realize that it was because it smelled like Craxan. She took a deep breath and sighed happily, then ducked into the bathroom for a quick wash before pulling the dress over her head.

The design was simple, a straight fall of cloth from her shoulders to her ankles, but he had managed to drape the neckline into a flattering cowl and the matching ribbon that tied beneath her breasts accentuated her curvy figure.

"You look beautiful, Mama," Tavi said, her eyes wide. "Like a princess."

"You're the princess, sweetheart."

"We'll both be princesses! Right, Papa?" Her daughter turned to address Craxan as he entered. "Don't we look nice?"

"Very nice," he agreed as he bent down to pick her up. She curled her tiny arm around his neck and smiled triumphantly.

"Perhaps too nice," he added, and Joanna saw his eyes were

focused on the subtle swell of breasts at the neckline of her dress. She knew that heated look all too well, and her nipples tightened against the cool silk.

"You should wear your cloak."

His possessiveness caused an atavistic thrill, her clit pulsing with excitement. Oh, Lord, she was ready for the evening to be over before it even began.

"I'm not going to do anything of the sort. I have you to watch over me, don't I?"

"Alwa—" He choked off his words. "We should go."

He had been about to say always, she was sure of it. Why had he stopped? Because this was only a job?

But he seemed to recognize her doubts, his tail curving comfortingly around her waist.

"I will look after you," he promised.

It wasn't always, but he was here now. She leaned into him and patted his tail.

"You look nice too, Papa," Tavi said, and Joanna noticed for the first time that he was wearing a new shirt. Dark green rather than black, it stretched across his massive chest with a lustrous gleam.

His skin actually seemed to darken along his prominent cheekbones. "I borrowed the shirt from Jed. It is a little tight."

"I don't have any objection to that," she murmured, and his tail dropped down to pat her bottom. Mmm, base three point five.

Captain Merios was waiting for them in the dining room. She recognized his mocking voice from their first encounter, but she could also see a faint resemblance to Rissta, which made her feel more comfortable. She liked the elderly female, despite her brusque demeanor.

"My, my. I see why your... mate has chosen to hide you away," he drawled.

She didn't like the hint of doubt in the way he said mate, but she smiled pleasantly. "I haven't been hiding. I've been working. Perhaps that is not a concept with which you are familiar?"

He gave her a stunned look, then started to laugh, fangs flashing. "I believe you have been spending entirely too much time with my grandmother."

"Nonsense. The girl simply knows a wastrel when she sees one," Rissta said tartly as she appeared, leading a robotic food cart.

"I'm sure you're correct, Grandmother," he agreed as he went to assist her.

"You should have worn your cloak," Craxan muttered, pulling her closer.

She laughed and shook her head. But then another male entered, Anaeus, the cargo master, and the way he looked at her made her feel uncomfortably exposed. He reached for her hand, but Craxan growled and stepped between them.

"Remember what I said."

Craxan's tone was deadly, and she suddenly remembered that brief fight back on Alliko. He might be sweet and kind and wonderful to them, but he had another side.

"Just like the beast, Mama," Tavi whispered excitedly.

"Yes, sweetheart. Our beast."

Yengik came in next, followed by Craxan's friend Jed. He had a distinctly snakelike appearance with slit-pupiled eyes and a forked tongue. His skin was covered with smooth, shimmering scales, but she much preferred the rougher texture of Craxan's skin.

"I am honored to meet you, Mate of Craxan." He bowed gracefully, but didn't try to take her hand.

"Umm, why don't you just call me Joanna?"

Jed shot a glance at Craxan and when Craxan nodded, he bowed his head. "I am honored."

The two remaining members of the crew were a mated pair of Kissats. The engineer, Sayla, was a slender, quiet male, while his partner Hagrin, the navigator, was loud and jovial.

Dinner turned out to be surprisingly pleasant. The captain was an entertaining conversationalist, especially combined with his grandmother's acerbic asides. Yengik didn't speak much, but he kept Tavi entertained. The others chatted amicably, only Anaeus not participating in the general conversation. He was seated at the other end of the big table, but she could feel him watching her and it made her skin crawl.

The food was given lavish praise, but she watched their reactions as they ate as well. On the whole their actions matched their words, but Jed pushed most of a leafy green to one side of his plate and Hagrin discreetly added more spice to his food.

As the meal drew to a close, the captain passed around small crystal glasses filled with a deep red liquid. He didn't offer it to either Tavi or Yengik, and when he came to Jed, he raised a mocking eyebrow.

"Farlan brandy?"

"No. Thank you."

Merios shrugged and moved on, and she saw Jed's hand twitch.

The brandy was strong, but delicious, and she could feel it warming her insides. Contentment filled her.

And then Merios spoke.

"We will land on Driguera tomorrow morning, ship time. It will be close to midnight on the surface and I wish to undertake the job immediately."

Driguera. The memory of Craxan telling her that it might

be dangerous swept over her, and she found herself clutching his tail.

"What is Driguera?" she asked, trying to keep her voice from shaking.

"It is a... trading port." The captain's eyes were unexpectedly kind, and it made her feel even worse.

"It is a hot bed of scum and villainy, filled with bastards who would just as soon knife you as look at you. It has the highest murder rate in the sector," Anaeus said, smirking.

"Leave now." Merios's voice turned deadly. "And I may decide to let you remain on board."

Anaeus shrugged, but he rose to his feet. "Remember, you need me."

The obnoxious male left, but her pulse was racing so fast that she felt dizzy. She darted a glance at Tavi, but her daughter only looked puzzled. Either she hadn't heard or she didn't understand what was happening.

"I'm going to take this little one back to my cabin," Rissta announced, rising to her feet. "I have some games she will like. And I might even be able to find a few sweets."

Tavi's face lit up. "Can I go, Mama?"

"Yes, but not too many sweets." Her lips felt numb, but her voice must have sounded normal because Tavi only grinned happily.

"You too, Yengik," Rissta ordered.

The three of them left, followed by Sayla and Hagrin, and Craxan immediately turned to her.

"Do not worry, my mate."

"Don't worry? What if something happens to you?" she cried, then turned to Merios. "Was Anaeus wrong?"

"Not exactly." He swirled the liquor in his glass, not looking at her.

"Then don't do it, don't go. Don't make Craxan go."

THE NANNY AND THE ALIEN WARRIOR

"It is necessary." The captain's expression hardened. "And it is the price that we agreed on for your passage."

"But I—"

"Do not worry, my mate," Craxan said soothingly. "I told you that I could take care of myself."

His attempt to calm her only added anger to her increasing panic. She wrenched herself free of his tail and raced out of the room, then realized she didn't know where Rissta's cabin was located. And perhaps it was better that Tavi didn't see her when she was this upset. She would get herself under control and then get her daughter.

But control did not come that easily. She paced back and forth in their small room as more and more nightmarish scenarios filled her head, then collapsed onto the bench, trying to hold back the tears.

"May I come in?" Craxan stood in the doorway, his face stern.

"Since you're willing to barter your life for a cabin, I'm not going to try and keep you out of it," she snapped.

He sighed and came in, sitting silently at the other end of the bench. His tail kept flicking towards her, but it didn't make contact and she actually missed the comforting touch.

"I don't want you to go," she burst out.

"I know, but I gave my word."

"We can find another way to pay for the cabin. Maybe I could take over as cook for the rest of the voyage."

"I suspect Rissta would have something to say about that," he said dryly. "My mate, I promise you, I am very good at what I do."

"But everyone makes mistakes."

"Do you think I do not know that? I made a mistake when I let my stubborn pride come between me and Vanha. But if I had been with him, he would not have died. Look at me," he said gently, and at last his tail curved around her wrist. "Do I not look like a capable warrior?"

She had to admit he did. The tight, gleaming fabric of his borrowed shirt accentuated his broad shoulders and massive chest. The usual softness in his expression had vanished and his features were hard, fierce in the dim light.

"I suppose," she said reluctantly.

His tail stroked her arm soothingly. "And although I do not expect it to happen, if something should... prevent me from returning to you, I have asked Jed to take care of you."

"Jed?"

"Yes. He is a worthy—"

"You expect me to let some man I don't even know swoop in and replace you? Did you tell him to hold me too? To touch me?"

"Never," he roared. "You are mine, Joanna. No one will ever touch you except me."

They stared at each other in the deafening silence following his cry. She couldn't tell who moved first, but then she was in his arms. His mouth devoured her frantically, and her response was just as urgent. He shoved the top of her dress down, groaning into her mouth as her breasts filled his hands. Strong fingers clamped down on her nipples, harder than he usually touched her, but the sharp pinch sent a shockwave of excitement straight to her clit.

He bent her back over his arm, taking her nipple in his mouth while his other hand slid beneath her dress, seeking the damp heat between her thighs. When he found the swollen pearl of her clit, she shuddered, trying to muffle her cry.

"Let me hear your pleasure," he demanded, deliberately swirling his finger over the sensitive flesh.

"Craxan," she cried, already quivering on the edge of climax.

He growled approvingly. "Now I want to see this pretty cunt, all slick and ready for me."

Her dress disappeared in a flutter of silk, and then she was naked. He lifted his head and looked down at her, running his hand from the fullness of her breast to the curve of her hip.

"You are beautiful, my mate."

"I want to see you too." He'd never removed his pants or allowed her more than a brief, tantalizing caress of his cock.

He obeyed immediately, stripping off his shirt and pants with astonishing speed.

Oh my.

Somehow he looked even bigger without his clothes, all his muscles clearly defined and rippling as he bent back down over her. And his cock... long and thick and covered with the same small nubs that patterned his skin.

Her pussy clenched so hard that she gasped. She reached for him, but he knelt between her legs instead. Her cheeks flamed as he spread her legs, his eyes focused on her exposed folds.

"Beautiful," he murmured again, then leaned closer and swiped his tongue from her entrance to her clit in one long stroke.

She could feel each nub sliding across the sensitive skin, even as his tail came up to probe at her entrance. He had done this before, but in the dark and under her shirt when she could not cry out. The fact that he could see everything now added to her excitement, and when he curled his tongue around her clit and tugged, she came with a hoarse cry. Her pussy fluttered wildly around his tail, but he was already pulling it free.

"I cannot wait any longer," he growled, and pulled her straight down onto his cock.

Her body shook, overwhelmed by the sudden shocking fullness. He was so deep inside her that she felt as if they were one, even as her clenching channel tried desperately to adjust to his size. But then he reached down and swept his thumb across her clit, exposed and throbbing, and she came again, her body convulsing over and over as she tried to tighten around the massive intruder.

When she recovered enough to notice her surroundings, she realized he was panting, his hands clenched on her hips, and his body rigid.

"Are you all right?" she whispered.

"All right? I had never thought to experience such pleasure. To feel your sweet cunt gripping me so tightly. To know that you are mine." He focused on her face, his black eyes burning. "You are mine, Joanna. I claim you as my mate."

It was not a question, but she nodded. "Yes, Craxan. I'm yours."

His hands tightened, and then his stillness vanished. He lifted her slightly, then thrust back into her, and now she could feel his nubs, rubbing against every sensitive inch of her channel. His speed increased, raising and lowering her over his cock with desperate urgency, and she did her best to meet every stroke. Her hands tightened on his shoulders, her nails biting into his skin, and he groaned and moved faster. A hoarse cry erupted from his lips as he slammed her down one last time. The base of his cock expanded, the impossible stretch sending her into yet another climax as the heated rush of his seed filled her completely.

She collapsed against his chest and his arms came around her, holding her as if he would never let her go. And she never wanted to leave him.

"How long will this last?" she whispered.

"The knotting? I am not sure. I have never done this before. I told you, it only occurs with our true mate."

His eyes were warm, amused, but then she wiggled a little,

experimentally, and heat flared. Her channel was still trying to adjust, and even the slight movement sent little shocks of electricity through the sensitive flesh.

"So we have to wait?" she gasped.

"Wait? Oh no." His thumb stroked across her clit again as his tail probed delicately at her bottom hole. Excitement shivered down her spine as he growled. "We do not have to wait at all."

CHAPTER ELEVEN

Once again, Craxan had not slept, holding Joanna tightly against his chest after she succumbed to an exhausted slumber. He had been truthful with his mate—he was not particularly worried about escorting the captain to pick up his mysterious cargo. But he still hated that he would have to leave her, especially now that they were truly bonded.

His mind replayed the events of the evening over and over. How beautiful she looked without clothing, her soft curves glowing in the warm light. The exquisitely tight clasp of her sweet cunt. The small gasp she gave when he touched her just right. The trust in her eyes when she looked at him while they were locked together.

His cock was as hard as if he had not knotted inside her twice already, experiencing an ecstasy he had never thought to receive.

When his internal alarm warned him that it was time to go, he hesitated. Should he wake her from her peaceful slumber or just leave her a note? He longed to taste her lips again, but which would be easier for her?

In the end, he did not have to decide. As soon as he slipped his arm out from under her, her eyes fluttered open. She looked up at him, her eyes dark and solemn, then pressed a hand to his face.

"Come back to me."

"Always," he said just as he had longed to do the previous day.

Her lips trembled, but she smiled at him.

"Should I go and tell Tavi goodbye?" he asked.

She thought for a moment, then shook her head. "I think it would worry her more."

"Very well." Time was passing, but it was difficult to tear himself away. "I will miss you, my mate."

He could see the sparkle of tears in her eyes. "I'll miss you too, but please don't say it so seriously. It makes me think this is goodbye."

"It is not goodbye," he promised.

"Good." She managed a smile. "Because I wanted to try base four point one again."

His cock jerked reflexively. "You are making it very difficult to leave."

"Consider it a reason to return," she said.

He could tell she was trying to tease him, even though her voice trembled, and he played along.

"I will. Because I have also been considering four point two."

His tail traced the soft curve of her ass, and she gave a breathless laugh as he finally pulled away. "I can see we have a lot to explore."

"Just think of that, and I will be back before you know it."

He kissed her again, far too quickly, then pulled on his uniform. As he reached the door, he turned back to look at her.

She deliberately lowered the sheet to reveal her luscious breasts and circled one rosy nipple.

"I'm considering the possibilities for four point three," she told him, then laughed when he tripped over his own feet.

He made his way out of the cabin and found Jed waiting for him.

"You're sure about this?" the other male asked.

"You are as bad as my mate," he growled. "I gave my word."

"I know. I just wish we knew more about the captain. Every time I think I have him figured out, he does something that makes me doubt my assumptions."

Merios was somewhat of a mystery, but he did not believe the male was malicious. Of course, that did not mean that he was not going to the situation with an abundance of caution.

"You will watch over my mate and child while I am gone."

"Of course."

The captain was waiting in the cargo hold, and he raised a sardonic eyebrow as they approached. "I'm terribly sorry if this job interrupted your slumber. Or perhaps you weren't only sleeping?"

He knew Merios was just taunting him, punishing him for being late, and he refused to give him the satisfaction of revealing his annoyance.

"Are we leaving, or are you just going to stand there talking to yourself?"

Merios scowled at him, and turned to Jed. "Lock the ship. No one goes in or out until we return."

"Yes, Captain."

"Can I rely on you?"

Jed lifted his chin and met the other male's eyes. "Yes, Captain."

Somewhat to Craxan's surprise, Merios accepted Jed's assurance without further comment. He turned and led the way down the small personnel ramp. As soon as they reached the bottom, he set it to retreat into the ship.

The usual sense of disorientation washed over Craxan as they crossed the landing field in the dark, but he was used to making the transition from ship time to planet time. By the time they reached the stalls that ringed the field, he had adjusted his internal clock.

Although he had heard of Driguera, he had never been here before. He kept his face impassive as he followed the captain, but his eyes constantly searched for any signs of danger. At least outwardly, Driguera did not appear any worse than any other rather seedy spaceport, although it was significantly larger.

They traveled through streets lined with more stalls, selling everything from food to mechanical tools to highly illegal substances. Even at this late hour, the streets were full of people going about their business. Most of them were armed, he noted, and there were few females other than the occasional pleasure companion.

As they traveled deeper into the port, the streets grew quieter. Retail establishments, heavily barred, were closed for the night. The bars, of course, were not. A fight broke out as they passed one, and a strange male came at them with a knife for no apparent reason other than because they were there. Craxan intercepted him and knocked him to the ground, leaving him clutching a broken wrist and screaming obscenities.

"I knew you were the right male for the job," Merios said casually as they moved into a more residential section.

A group of males loitering on a street corner looked them over, but must have decided they weren't worth the effort because they didn't bother them. The houses grew larger and more prosperous, until they finally emerged on a street lined with enormous townhouses, packed shoulder to shoulder along each side.

"That's the one," Merios said quietly, gesturing at one of the largest houses.

The building was typical for wealthy city dwellers. Ornate frescoes decorated the façade, and tall windows lined the upper floors. However, the ground floor had no windows or doors, only a gated tunnel that led through into an inner courtyard. The actual living quarters were only accessible from that courtyard.

Two neatly uniformed guards stood on either side of the tunnel, their eyes alert. Professionals. Merios strolled up to them as casually as if he were walking onto his own ship.

"I am Captain Merios. I have an appointment with Lord Rulmat."

"And the Cire?"

"Protection. For the product."

One guard laughed unpleasantly. "How the Cire have fallen. Hired help for a pirate captain."

Craxan did not bother to respond. Insults did not damage him.

The guard looked disappointed at his lack of response, but he opened the gate and led them down the tunnel, while the other guard remained at his post. Craxan caught the glint of security cameras in the roof of the tunnel, turning to follow their progress.

Elaborate stone mosaics formed the floor of the inner courtyard, with small scented plants artfully arranged around a central pool. But despite the trappings of wealth, the space was designed for defense. Guards on the upper level would have an unobscured view of the entire area. There were no places for an assassin to lie concealed, nowhere for an enemy to shelter.

A chill shivered down his spine. Just who were they meeting?

A four-story building formed one side of the courtyard, the only access a narrow stairway with two guards at the bottom and one at the top. A lower building at the rear of the courtyard was no doubt intended for the guards and the household staff, while the side walls were sheer stone, covered with decorative tiles. Overhead, the night sky had the faintest shimmer, an indication of a protective shield covering the courtyard. The place was a fortress.

The gate guard passed them off to the stairway guards, one of whom followed them up the stairs. At the top of the stairs, the atmosphere changed completely. Lush plantings divided a wide veranda into numerous seating areas, the furniture carved from rare woods and heaped with cushions covered in the finest fabrics. There was no evidence of further security, although he had no doubt it existed.

He followed silently as the guard led them into a great hall with a towering ceiling. The tall windows he had seen from the street lined one side of the room, currently covered with heavy drapes, while the remaining walls were paneled with more exotic woods. The surroundings were designed to impress, but he was more interested in the male lounging next to an actual fire. Like most heavily populated planets, open combustion had been banned on Driguera many years ago. The fact that the male had no hesitation in flaunting the law confirmed his suspicions. Only a very powerful criminal—or a politician—would dare to behave in such a manner.

The male was a Skaal like Jed, but completely different from his friend. His well-oiled scales shimmered in the firelight, covering a body that was no longer in its prime, but still heavily muscled. Small gold piercings outlined his features, then continued down his chest in a series of elaborate designs, visible beneath the open silk robe.

"Captain Merios," the male drawled. "At last."

"I apologize, Lord Rulmat. I encountered some unexpected delays." The captain's words were polite enough, but the sardonic note was more apparent than usual.

"I was considering cancelling our transaction, but since you are here—do you have my credits?"

Merios held up a gold credit chit. "But of course, I wish to inspect the product first."

"Of course. This way."

Rulmat rose to his feet in a single powerful move, then led the way out of the room to a narrow set of stairs tucked in an outside corner. As soon as they were below the main level, the elaborate paneling disappeared, replaced by rough stone walls. At the bottom of the stairs, Rulmat unlocked a door and ushered them through into a stark, dimly lit corridor. The air smelled of blood and violence, and Craxan's tail lashed anxiously.

Despite his finery, Rulmat looked at home in this dark basement, perhaps even more than he had in the riches above, and Craxan grew increasingly suspicious of the reason for their trip.

"The product is in here." Rulmat unlocked a dirty yellow door.

The only light came from the hallway behind them, and it took a moment for Craxan's eyes to adjust. Outrage roared through him as he saw the figure chained to the far wall. Human. Female. And painfully young, he realized as he took in the pale, dirty face behind the gag. A bruise discolored one cheek, but her eyes blazed defiantly at him.

He started to turn, to seize the worthless male by the throat —and Merios pressed a blaster against his back.

A shot in that specific spot would be instantly fatal, but he would have chanced it anyway if it was not for Joanna and Sultavi. The bastard was dealing in slaves. He had to make it back to the ship before the captain could add the two of them to his cargo. How could he have been so stupid as to trust the other male?

"Not in the best condition," Merios drawled, and Craxan's tail lashed with suppressed rage, as he waited for his opportunity to kill both males.

Rulmat shrugged. "She cleans up all right. If you like that kind of thing."

"Yet you want to get rid of her?"

"I got what I wanted. And I'm tired of the constant defiance."

"Which also lessens the value."

"Not necessarily. Some males enjoy it." Rulmat's fangs flashed as he leered at Merios. "I've even heard that Kissat males like a good tussle."

Did the fur spike on the captain's shoulders? He couldn't tell in the uncertain light.

"Occasionally," Merios drawled, but his voice sounded strained.

"Anyway, we have already agreed on a price. Are you changing your mind?" Rulmat raised a pierced brow. "I have plenty of other buyers interested."

"No. We will take her away from you." The captain tapped the blaster meaningfully against Craxan's back as he spoke, then let it drop. Did his words have an underlying meaning?

Despite the rage still sizzling in his veins, he also realized that Merios had made sure the other male could not see the blaster. He forced himself to remain quiet and await additional information.

"Off this planet," Rulmat insisted. "That was the arrangement."

"We're heading for the underground market on Regten," Merios drawled. "Is that far enough?"

Craxan managed to keep his face impassive, even though Regten was in the opposite direction from Trevelor. However, the female struggled even more wildly, her muffled protests muted by the gag.

The captain sighed. "Do you have a cloak? I do not wish to attract attention, and I suspect she will not come quietly."

"There should be something in the room at the end of the corridor. Your Cire can fetch it while we conclude our business."

Merios nodded, shooting him what looked like a warning look. His anger had cooled to the point where he suspected there was more to this encounter than his original impression, so he jerked an assent and obeyed. All he could find was a ripped and none too clean blanket, but it was better than nothing.

He returned just as the other two completed the transaction.

"Remember," Rulmat said. "Off planet. If I hear that you decided to pick up a quick profit at the local market instead, I will not be pleased."

His previous affability had vanished, his voice low and deadly, confirming Craxan's earlier suspicions. Rulmat was more than just a wealthy merchant with a penchant for human females.

"We're leaving immediately," Merios assured him, then turned to Craxan. "Bring the female."

Rulmat manipulated a wall control and the chains retracted. The female crumpled to the floor. Her ankles and wrists were still bound, and he bent to untie them.

"If you do not want to attract attention, you will not release her." Rulmat had resumed his previous mocking tone.

Craxan shot a look at Merios, and the captain nodded grimly. Perhaps he was right. There were far too many unsavory individuals walking the streets of Driguera to take the chance.

"This is for your own good," he murmured softly as he wrapped the blanket around the female, covering her completely, then placed her over his shoulder as gently as possible.

He hated it. Not only did he hate the entire situation, but he hated carrying any female other than his mate. His skin crawled from the touch of another female, and her smell irritated his scent receptors. It was all he could do to keep his face impassive as they climbed back up the stairs.

The guards jeered at them as they left, but didn't interfere.

As soon as they were two blocks away from the house, he pulled Merios into a shadowed doorway.

"Now tell me what the hell is going on," he demanded.

CHAPTER TWELVE

Merios sighed. "Put her down, and I will tell both of you."

Craxan put the squirming female on her feet and pulled back the blanket to reveal her face. Her eyes still blazed, and she immediately tried to make a run for it, but her feet were still bound and she only tripped forward. Merios caught her.

"Stop struggling," he ordered quietly. "We are not the enemy. We are going to take you away from here, to a place where you can be free."

If anything, her struggles increased, and Merios gave Craxan a frustrated glance. "You have more experience with human females than I do. What is her problem?"

"She probably does not believe you. I am not sure that I do. Why did you not tell me?"

"Would you have accompanied me if I told you I was going to buy a slave?"

"Perhaps not," he admitted. He still hated the idea that Rulmat had profited from the sale of a female. "You should have called in the Patrol."

"It's too dangerous. If something had gone wrong and Rulmat had received word, he would have eliminated her."

"So you are on a mission to free slaves?" he asked dubiously.

Merios sighed. "No. But I have a relative who has made it his cause. He occasionally asks me to, err, pick one up. I purchase them, and once I have them safely away from the planet, he sends in the Patrol."

"That seems somewhat... uncharacteristic."

"I assure you he pays me quite well." The captain glared at the female who had stopped struggling as she listened to them, her eyes darting between their faces. "But they are usually more grateful."

"She might be if you untied her," he said dryly.

"I suppose you're right." Merios pulled out his knife, and the female immediately renewed her efforts. "Stop that, you foolish female."

The captain bent down and cut the ankle bindings, and she kicked him, her foot hitting his thigh with an audible thud. He glared at her, then at Craxan. "Can you hold her while I cut the others? We are trying not to attract attention, remember?"

He was tempted to let her wreak whatever damage she could on the arrogant male, but Merios was right, they did not want anyone to investigate. He gripped her arms, gently but firmly, as Merios first released her hands, then removed her gag.

"Let me go," she hissed.

"Don't be ridiculous." Merios scowled at her. "Someone would have you back in captivity within minutes."

She glared at the other male, then her body went completely limp and she slid towards the ground. Craxan tried to adjust his grip, and she suddenly twisted free, racing away from them. She was fast, but he was faster, and he grabbed her again before she reached the end of the alley.

"What are you doing?" He realized she had been heading back towards the house they had just left. "You wish to return to him?"

"Never," she spat. "But I'm not leaving without my son."

"He has your child?" The knowledge horrified him.

"That's what he meant when he said he had what he wanted." Merios gave him a grim look as he joined them and heard her words.

"And why he was so insistent that you take her off the planet."

"Yeah. He's trying to get rid of me. As soon as I got pregnant, he lost interest. He just wanted a son. But Adam is mine," she said fiercely. "That bastard can't have him."

They exchanged looks over her head, then Merios sighed.

"We have to go back."

"I know." He knew what he needed to do, even though the words wanted to stick in his throat. By Granthar, Merios had better deserve his trust. "Take her back to the ship. I will get the child."

"By yourself?"

"Infiltration is my specialty." He turned to the girl. "Can you tell me where your son is kept?"

"He has a suite on the top floor. I was taken there at first, to feed him, but then they decided he didn't need me anymore." She crossed her arms over her breasts, a single tear sliding down her cheek. "But he does! Can you really get him out?"

"Yes."

"I... I can't pay you. Not in credits. But I could..." Her hand shook, but she reached for the fastening on his pants.

"No!" He jerked back so quickly that his back hit the wall. "I have a mate. But even if I did not, I would not accept such a payment."

"I almost believe you mean that," she said, studying his face. "But please, please bring me my son."

"I will," he promised, then took a step closer to Merios, looming over him as his voice turned deadly. "I am putting my trust in you. If you allow any harm to come to my family, I will not rest until I destroy you and everything you care about."

Merios met his eyes, the mockery completely absent for once. "You have my word."

"Then I will meet you at the ship."

Craxan turned and strode quickly through the dark streets. Thoughts of Joanna and Sultavi kept dancing through his mind, and he finally had to stop and force himself to take some deep, calming breaths. He had made the decision to trust Merios. No matter how difficult, he had to put his faith in the other male and concentrate on his job.

An approach from the front of the building was out of the question - the tunnel was too well guarded. In his experience, the entrances used by the staff were much less protected. The wealthy were far less concerned about the members of their household and assumed, with some justification, that an intruder would be deterred by a barracks full of guards.

Craxan was not so easily discouraged.

The alley that ran behind the back of the row of wealthy houses was not difficult to find. Even at this hour it bustled with activity—men returning from an evening's entertainment, vendors delivering products for the next day, even a few pleasure companions looking for some last credits. He pulled his cloak over his head and kept to the shadows, but he knew he wouldn't look out of place amongst the guards.

The back of Lord Rulmat's house was just as he had hoped. Not one, but two doors led out into the alley. Both were open, light spilling out onto the pavement. In one, a guard bargained with a pleasure companion. The other appeared unoccupied.

As the guard at the first door began unfastening his pants, Craxan slipped through the unguarded entrance. Off to one side, he caught sight of the guard who should have been watching the doorway taking a piss. He shook his head as he slipped silently along the corridor. Incompetence made his job so much easier.

He could hear voices from many of the rooms as he found the stairs and began to climb, but the staff was settling down for the night and he was able to avoid the other inhabitants. Until he came to the stairs that led to the roof and found an all too awake guard.

The guard's eyes widened at the sight of Craxan and his mouth opened, but the moment of surprise was enough. His tail lashed out, throwing the male off balance, and he had his arm around the male's throat before he could cry out. He was tempted to break the guard's neck, but despite the male's presence in such an unsavory household, he had no real proof that he had caused harm to others. He settled for rendering him unconscious, then slid his body into a nearby storage closet.

Reaching the roof took only seconds, but the next part would be more difficult. He would need to make his way across one of the side walls and over to the main house. He should be beneath the protective shield, but he would be exposed if anyone chose to look up. Fortunately, very few people ever raised their eyes.

His dark, close-fitting uniform would be less conspicuous than his cloak, so he let it slip free, then took the first step out onto the wall. Despite the steep drop, he strode quickly along the wall, his footsteps sure and his tail providing additional balance. Just as he reached the main building, he heard shouts from below. Had he been seen?

He slipped into the shadow of a window, his heart pounding. He had done this type of thing many times before, and he had never succumbed to nerves. But this time Joanna and Sultavi were waiting for him, and he had so much more to lose. His hands were actually shaking as he risked a glance down below.

A small group of guards was crouched over a dice game, and one of them was clearly a big winner. His companions jeered and shook their heads as he grinned triumphantly. Someone came out onto the veranda below and yelled at them to keep quiet, and the noise faded away immediately.

Craxan's heart slowed to its normal rhythm, but as he searched for the stairs leading up to the top floor, he thought about his reaction. He had never been reckless, but neither had he been overly concerned about the risks he took. Yet another sign that he needed a different profession.

The upper floor lay in hushed stillness. A long corridor led the length of the house, ending in a pair of ornate doors. He was willing to bet that Rulmat slept behind those doors. Four other doors opened onto the corridor, and he swore silently that he had not asked the female for more information. Yet another sign that his edge had slipped.

He considered the options, then decided that Rulmat was not the type who would enjoy being disturbed by a crying child. He chose the door farthest from the bedroom and slipped quietly inside.

He found a large room, filled with elaborate toys, and couldn't help thinking how much Sultavi would have enjoyed them. She deserved to be in such luxurious surroundings. *But not at the cost of such a parent*, he reminded himself.

Another set of doors opened into an inner room. A small night light burned next to a heavily gilded crib, while an elderly Skaal female slept in a chair by the window, snoring quietly. He crept across the room and looked down at the child. Pale blue scales shimmered in the dim light, but his features were human, and he had a tuft of fine, dark hair on his head.

He reached down and carefully gathered the sleeping child into his arms, so tiny and fragile. As he turned back towards the door, he saw the female was awake. Tension filled the room as they stared at each other. He should silence her before she could call for help, but he could not bring himself to do so.

"I am returning the child to his mother," he said softly.

She studied him, then nodded. "Good."

"You will not raise the alarm?"

"No."

He believed her. He took a step towards the door, then turned back. "Will you be harmed when they discover he is gone?"

"My daughter was his mate, but when she could not give him a child, he made her suffer until she just... faded away. Now he will be the one to suffer." Her lips twisted, but it was not a smile. "I will enjoy that, no matter what he does to me."

"You could accompany me." He knew it was a risky offer, but he hated the thought of leaving her here with a male like Rulmat.

This time she did smile. "You're a foolish male. We both know I would only increase the chance that you would be caught, and I would rather know that the child is free. He is a sweet boy."

She put her head against the back of the chair and closed her eyes.

"You are sure?"

"Go," she said without opening her eyes.

He went.

The trip back across the wall went even more quickly this time. He was painfully aware of the slight weight against his chest, praying that the infant would not wake and cry out. On the other side, he picked up his still undisturbed cloak, then considered his options. A burst of raucous laughter from below made the child twitch, but he did not come fully awake. Nonetheless, that confirmed his decision not to try and return through the building.

He had spotted another possibility earlier, and now he hurried to the window overlooking the alley. An old-fashioned pulley system, intended to lift large objects to the upper floors, hung in a shaft to his left. That would work.

He climbed out of the window, bracing himself against the sill for a moment before leaping for the chain. His free hand caught it, slipped, and then his tail grabbed hold. Deep shadows concealed the shaft, but once again, he trusted that no one would look up as he made his way swiftly and silently down the chain. It ended a considerable distance above the ground. Knowing that he would have to jump, he hung there, his arm aching, until more laughter erupted and he dropped silently to the ground.

Between the shadows and the distraction, no one had noticed him. He glanced down at his precious burden, and saw the child looking silently up at him. His eyes were human, the same rich brown as his mate's, but there was a watchfulness there that seemed wrong on an infant. Had he already learned not to cry out?

"You are safe now," he whispered, his tail curling protectively around the small figure.

The infant blinked, then his eyes closed and his body relaxed. Still holding him securely with his tail, he pulled his cloak closed and set off down the alley. He wanted to hurry, but he forced himself to nothing more than the brisk pace of a male about his business. No one paid any attention to him, although an inebriated guard gave him a startled look when he stumbled into him.

"Thorry," the male mumbled, looking confused. "Say, aren't you that Thire?"

"No," he said curtly, and kept moving.

Fuck. Hopefully the idiot was too drunk to remember him.

As soon as he was clear of the alley, he increased his pace. He still could not run, but his strides were rapid enough that he reached the ship just as Merios and the female were about to board.

"Why are you here already?" she demanded, panic covering her face. "You promised—"

"Here." He opened his cloak and passed her the infant.

"Adam," she whispered, snatching him away from Craxan. Tears streamed down her cheeks, and he saw her legs start to buckle.

With a resigned sigh, he caught her before she fell, and then started up the landing ramp. "We need to leave."

"Agreed." Merios was right behind him, pausing only long enough to close the ramp.

As soon as they were on board, he put the female and the child down, but she clung to his arm, still sobbing, even though he tried to remove her hand.

"I can't believe you got him back. I can't ever thank you enough. I'll do anything you want, anything."

"Oh, really?" Joanna's voice dropped the temperature in the cargo hold at least ten degrees. "Just what do you want her to do, Craxan?"

CHAPTER THIRTEEN

Jealousy raged through Joanna as she saw the half-naked girl clinging to Craxan. He'd left her here at the ship to worry her brains out so he could bring another woman on board? A dirty but undeniably attractive girl, her breasts spilling out of her torn dress as she cradled a child—*a child?*

Her thoughts came to an abrupt halt as logic finally overcame her jealousy. The girl clinging to Craxan was human. She even looked vaguely familiar...

"Suzanna?"

"Professor Wilder?" The girl stared at her in shock, then flinched and looked away. "They took you too?"

She had been the one struggling under the trees, Joanna realized.

"Yes. What hap—" She stopped mid-sentence. From the girl's condition and the half alien child in her arms, what had happened was all too clear.

Instead, she turned to Merios. "This is why we stopped here?"

"They bought me," Suzanna said softly.

"They did what?" Outrage filled her, and she stalked over and put a protective arm around the girl and her child.

Craxan opened his mouth, but Merios beat him to it.

"It was the only way to get her out of there. And unless you want her forced to return, we need to leave. Immediately."

"Why?" She glared at him suspiciously. "You said you bought her."

"We didn't buy the child."

"He went back for him." Suzanna gave Craxan another worshipful look. "He saved my son."

"He did, did he?"

She was glad the child had been freed, but she didn't appreciate the way the girl was looking at Craxan. To his credit, he looked uncomfortable, almost pained, and his tail was still trying to circle her wrist.

Meanwhile, Merios had slapped the communication panel and was issuing orders. Jed came hurrying into the cargo bay. Suzanna gave a muffled scream and tried to grab Craxan again.

"You're safe now," Joanna said, her voice tart, then felt ashamed of herself. She looked at Jed, then at the baby, and realized why the girl had panicked. She would be willing to bet that the father of the child had been of the same species.

Jed had frozen at the sight of Suzanna, his eyes also going from her to the baby. Then his shoulders straightened as he took a step forward.

"You have nothing to fear from me. I will never allow any harm to come to you or your child."

"And what in the world makes you think I'd take your word for that?" Suzanna glared at him, but she no longer looked as scared. She let go of Craxan, who immediately moved to Joanna's side.

"We're leaving," Merios ordered. "Is the ship ready?"

"Yes. Sayla is already in the engine room."

"Then take this female to the second guest cabin." Suzanna looked on the verge of panic again, and Merios sighed. "And show her how to lock the door."

The captain headed for the lift to the upper level, and the four of them looked at each other.

"Where is Sultavi?" Craxan asked.

"She's with Rissta. We should go and get her."

"In a minute. I need... to speak with you first."

He didn't sound like his usual self. His voice was strained and his face hard. Had something happened that he wasn't telling her about?

Despite her concern, she couldn't leave Suzanna with Jed when she was obviously uncomfortable in his presence.

"Why don't we all go up together?" she suggested.

The tension didn't ease as they made their way to the cabins. The one next to theirs had an identical layout, and she quickly showed Suzanna how to find all the hidden facilities. Craxan was pacing back and forth outside the door, his tail lashing furiously, while Jed stood silently nearby.

"I'll come back in a little while and we can figure out what else you need," she promised. "But I need to talk to Craxan first. Will you be all right?"

"As long as everyone leaves me alone," the girl said, glaring suspiciously at Jed.

"I will make sure you are undisturbed."

Suzanna looked skeptical, but she didn't argue. As soon as Joanna left, she heard the lock click behind her.

"I will—" Jed began, but she didn't hear the rest. Craxan's tail was around her waist and pulling her into their own cabin.

"What is it?" she asked anxiously. "What do you need to tell me?"

"I don't need to talk to you."

"But—"

"I just need you."

He stripped off his shirt, then sent his pants flying. Her mouth went dry at the sight of all those glorious muscles as he stalked towards her. He made short work of her clothes, and then her bare skin was pressed against his, the rough texture setting her nerves aflame.

He dipped his head to her neck, then growled and stepped back.

Her heart skipped a beat. "What's wrong?"

"I have to remove her scent. It is wrong."

"You could take a shower," she suggested reluctantly. She didn't want to let him out of her sight.

"An excellent idea." He scooped her up and carried her with him, then sent the shower liquid pouring down over both of them.

The bathroom was impossibly small with the two of them crowded in together, but she didn't care. Her whole body was on fire with longing.

"I need you." His voice was strained, his hands frantic as they roamed her body.

"How—"

Before she could finish the question, Craxan lifted her up against the wall, her back to the smooth metal. Her head brushed against the ceiling but she didn't care because his mouth was on her breasts, pulling on the sensitive peaks with almost painful intensity. She clutched his shoulders, squirming restlessly, seeking pressure against her needy clit.

He growled and reached between them, ripping away the thin fabric of her gown as he spread her legs further apart and yanked her towards him. She bit back a cry as he pressed her against the hard muscles of his chest, those marvelous nubs massaging her swollen flesh. His tail dove in between them, and she felt it probing at the entrance to her pussy just as he carefully scraped his teeth across an aching peak.

Her climax swept over her, shockingly intense, and she clamped down on her lip to avoid crying out as she shuddered in his arms. Before she could catch her breath, he slid her down his chest, each ridge of his abdomen sending another ripple of pleasure through her body and straight onto his cock. Oh my God. He seemed even bigger, even harder, and the nubs stroking her channel sent her straight into another climax, even as she struggled to adjust to his size.

His body was taut with strain, his muscles rigid, but he didn't move as she buried her face in his chest and tried to catch her breath. But then his tail swept across her clit, fully exposed, and her hips jerked towards him. He growled again, and then he was moving, yanking her frantically up and down the length of his shaft.

All she could do was hang on, her nails biting into his shoulders as sparks of excitement sizzled along her nerve endings with every thrust. Her nipples rubbed against his chest, a tantalizing counterpoint to the pressure against her swollen nub that added to her pleasure. His scent deepened until her head swam, and then he yanked her down hard, embedding himself as deeply as possible as a muffled roar escaped his mouth. He expanded inside her, locking them together as his heated seed flooded her channel, and she quivered in ecstasy.

His arms tightened around her as his head rested against her, and his weight pressed her against the wall, but she didn't mind. She felt safe and... loved.

"Thank you, my mate," he murmured, his voice hoarse.

"I think I'm the one who should be thanking you."

He raised his head and smiled down at her.

"It gives me great pleasure to know that you are satisfied."

"Very much so." She wiggled, testing the knot inside her, then gasped as he flexed in response and her own arousal flared.

"I am a fool," he said conversationally, tightening his arms.

"I don't believe that for a second."

"I am. I was blinded by the fact that I have spent my entire adult life in one profession."

"This really doesn't seem like the right time to discuss career choices." She shifted her position slightly and heard him groan.

"You do not understand. I want you, Joanna, you and Sultavi. I want you with me always. I have done since the moment I saw you outside the tavern."

Her heart skipped a beat. "You didn't say anything."

A big hand clamped down on her ass, drawing her even closer against him, and she gasped.

"I should have told you long ago, but I did not see how I could care for you. My profession pays well, but it is a specific skill and it would require me to travel."

She didn't like that idea at all. The few short hours when he'd been gone had been bad enough, but if he left for weeks at a time? And yet...

"I would rather have limited time with you than none at all," she whispered.

His hips jerked, his knot throbbing inside her, and she hovered on the brink of climax again.

"As would I, but I will find another profession. I love you, Joanna."

Happiness washed over her so quickly she felt dizzy. "I love you too."

He kissed her until she was breathless, then simply held her, and her heart overflowed with happiness.

A thought occurred to her. "Do you realize that you just told me you loved me for the first time in a bathroom?"

"Does that matter?"

She laughed. "No. But I'll have to come up with another story to tell our grandchildren."

"Grandchildren?"

"One day Sultavi will be mated, and hopefully she will have a child."

His eyes closed, the expression on his face almost pained.

"Craxan? What's wrong?"

"I never thought I would have a mate, let alone a child. Or grandchildren. It still seems like an impossible dream."

"It's not a dream. I'm here. Sultavi is here—metaphorically speaking. It's real." She suspected she was convincing herself as much as him. Even before she had been taken, she had decided that a family was not part of her future. And now she finally had one.

She ran her fingers along his jaw, her heart full. He was such a good male.

"As much as I love Tavi, I wish we could have children together. I would like to have had another child with you," she whispered.

A startled look crossed his face.

"What is it?"

"We were always told that a Cire could only mate with another Cire," he said slowly. "That it is only when we find our true mate and knot inside her that we become fertile." He looked down to where their bodies were locked together, his cock still buried deep inside. "But I am sure sure that you are my true mate and I knotted inside you."

A wild hope sprang to life in her heart, but she tried to push it down. They were so different, and she was no longer young.

"I'm not sure it's possible," she said, unable to keep her voice from shaking.

His tail cupped her chin, lifting her face to his. "It does not matter. If it should happen, I would be thrilled, of course. If it does not, then I will still be completely satisfied."

CHAPTER FOURTEEN

As much as Craxan would have liked to remain inside his mate, as soon as his knot subsided, he gently lifted her free. He washed her quickly, an awkward business in the tight space, but he did not mind and she voiced no objection.

"Let us find our daughter," he said as soon as they were dressed.

"She's still with Rissta. I joined them earlier but I was so nervous that she was starting to get worried."

They found Tavi in the kitchen, cheerfully cutting out pieces of dough, but she rushed over to him as soon as they entered. He swung her up in his arms, and she kissed his cheek.

"You're back. You've been gone forever and ever."

"I am afraid I had a job to do."

"But it's done now? You're not going away again?"

"Not permanently, but sometimes I will have to leave you while I work."

"Father had to work a lot too," she said sadly.

He saw Rissta shoot a look at him from under her brows, but he ignored her and concentrated on his daughter.

"I will be with you as much as I can," he promised, resolving to start investigating the possibility of a training job immediately.

"And Mama too?"

"And Mama too."

"Good. Do you want some of my bread?" She squirmed to be let down, then led him to the table.

"You made bread?"

"I did!"

"All by yourself?"

"Well, Miss Rissta helped a little." Her big eyes sparkled up at him, and he hugged her again as she proudly presented him with a slice of bread.

"She has a talent for it," Rissta admitted, then gave Joanna a thoughtful look. "Must take after her mother."

"Thank you," Joanna said calmly as she sat down with them.

Contentment filled him as they ate breakfast together. If every day could begin like this, he would be a happy male.

"I think I should go back and check on Suzanna now," Joanna said as they finished.

"And I need to talk to Merios."

"I'll meet you back here later," she promised as she kissed him. "Do you want to come with me, Tavi? We have a new passenger on board, and she has a baby."

"A girl?" Tavi asked eagerly.

"I am afraid he is a male child," he said solemnly.

"That's too bad," she sighed, and they all laughed as they went their separate ways.

He found Merios on the bridge, consulting with Hagrin.

"I was just going to send for you," the captain said cheerfully, and Craxan's suspicions flared.

"Why?"

"Slight change in plans. The ship is heading to Tyssia first."

"Isn't that uninhabited?"

Merios hesitated for a fraction of a second. "Yes. But my cousin has a station in orbit around it. I want to take the female and the child there."

"To a space station? It does not seem like an appropriate environment for a female and a child."

"I'm sure they won't be there long. He will arrange transportation for them."

He frowned at the captain. "You said we were going to Trevelor."

"And we will. After Tyssia." Merios shrugged. "Are you in a hurry?"

Was he? As much as he would like to prepare for their future, they were together now. "Perhaps not," he admitted. "Although I was looking forward to larger quarters."

"I might be able to arrange something."

"You never said that there were larger cabins available."

"We only made the deal for the small one." The other male's fangs glinted. "Are you really objecting?"

Object to the time spent snuggled together with his family in the tiny cabin? The forced proximity had brought them together. He had no complaints.

"No," he admitted. "But some additional space would be nice."

"There is a true family cabin across the hall from yours. I am willing to let you use it."

"And what do you want from me in return?" he asked suspiciously.

Merios shook his head. "So suspicious. I am… grateful that you went back for the child."

"I could not leave him."

"No. But some males would. Take the cabin."

"Very well. Thank you."

"There is one more thing," Merios added as Craxan turned to leave.

He sighed and turned back. "Why am I not surprised?"

"Jed informs me that Anaeus tried to leave the ship in Driguera. When I asked him, he said that he was trying to do some quick trading." The captain tapped his claws absently on the console. "I don't trust him—not that I ever did—but his recent behavior has been more concerning. He will be leaving the ship once we reach the station. I would like you to make sure that he does so peacefully, and with only his own belongings."

"Is that all?"

"Of course."

Merios was the picture of innocence, but Craxan decided the sooner they were off the ship the better. He suspected that the requests for his assistance would not stop as long as they were on board.

"And then Trevelor?"

"I said that was our ultimate destination."

"No, it will be our *next* destination," he said firmly.

"Very well. If you still wish to travel there, it will be our next stop."

"Why would we not want to go there?"

"You never know." Merios waved a casual hand. "Things can change."

"They will not," he said, and left the bridge before the captain made any more requests.

He headed for the exercise room, but found it empty.

Jed wasn't in the engine room or the crew quarters either. Craxan finally tracked him down in the small recreation room at the back of the ship. He was sitting in a worn chair, his eyes focused on a bottle on the table in front of him, his thumb rubbing back and forth over his fingers.

"Thank you for looking after my family," Craxan said as he sat down next to him.

"You're welcome." Jed's eyes never left the bottle.

"What's wrong?"

"Nothing."

Craxan kept silent, and Jed sighed. "Everything."

"That is comprehensive. Is it the female?"

"Yes," he burst out. "Did you see her? I don't mean to offend you, but when I met your mate, I decided that humans weren't a very attractive species. But Suzanna is the most beautiful creature I've ever seen. And her son is perfect."

"That does not sound like everything is wrong," he said mildly, suppressing his annoyance at Jed's dismissal of his mate.

"But she was abused." Jed's eyes looked haunted. "By a Skaal. She is afraid of me."

"The only way for her to grow less afraid is if she gets to know you. Which she cannot do if you are hiding in here."

"I thought perhaps a drink would help. Would calm my nerves so that I could speak to her."

He kept his face impassive. "And did it?"

"I don't know. I haven't taken a sip yet. Because that's how it starts."

"Can I help?"

"Yes." Jed grabbed the bottle and thrust it at Craxan. "Take it away and don't return it to me if I ask."

"Very well." He knew that it was no more than a symbolic gesture—alcohol was readily available on board—but if it would help his friend, then he would do what he could.

"Thank you."

"My mate is with Suzanna. Do you want to go with me?"

"I..." Jed straightened his shoulders and nodded. "Yes."

Joanna led Tavi back to Suzanna's cabin and knocked quietly. She didn't want to wake the other woman if she was sleeping.

"Who is it?"

"It's me, Joanna."

"Are you alone?"

"I have my daughter with me."

There was a short pause, and then the door slid open. Suzanna looked down at Tavi, then back at her, frowning.

"You said your daughter was with you, but she's far too old to be the result of—"

"She is the daughter of my heart," Joanna said firmly. "May we come in, or would you prefer to be alone?"

"Come in. When I'm alone it's too easy to think I'm still back there."

Tavi had been standing silently next to Joanna, looking at Suzanna.

"You need a bath," she said.

"Tavi, that's rude."

Suzanna bit her lip. "But it's the truth. I've been thinking about it, but I just didn't want to leave Adam. And... it was better to be dirty before."

Joanna would have put her hand on the girl's arm but she wasn't sure if the touch would be welcome. "We can watch Adam, if you would like."

The girl still hesitated. "Is the other snake man gone?"

"Do you mean Jed? I didn't see him."

Suzanna scowled. "He was lurking around outside the cabin. I told him to leave."

"He was just trying to watch over you," Joanna said gently.

"Well, I don't want him anywhere near me. He's too much

THE NANNY AND THE ALIEN WARRIOR

like—" Her fierce expression faded, and she shivered. "Never mind. If you'll watch the baby, I'll take that shower."

Tavi had already wandered over to the bench where Adam was sleeping. "He's awfully little."

"You were that little once too." Joanna smiled at her. "Babies have to be little so that they fit in their mama's tummies."

"Do you have one in your tummy now?"

Joanna shook her head, trying not to think about the possibility. She didn't want to get her hopes up. Suzanna opened her mouth, then glanced at Tavi and apparently reconsidered.

"I don't suppose there are any more clothes on board?" she asked wistfully.

"Not really, but I can lend you something. It will probably be too big."

"Better than being too small," the girl snorted, looking down at her skimpy outfit.

"I guess so. I'll be right back."

Joanna returned to their cabin and retrieved one of the outfits Craxan had made. As much as she hated to give it up, it would be selfish not to share. She had to remind herself again when Suzanna made a face when she took it.

"It smells kind of funny."

"I think it smells wonderful," she said fiercely, knowing Craxan's scent covered the cloth.

Suzanna bit her lip again. "Sorry. I didn't mean to offend you."

Joanna forced herself to smile. "I know you didn't. Now take your shower before this little one wakes up."

"Okay. Thanks."

Tavi was still studying the baby intently. "He would be prettier if he had green skin like Papa."

"I'm sure his mama loves him just the way he is, just like I love you just the way you are."

She sat down on the bench and Tavi climbed into her lap, then patted her stomach. "Are you sure there's no baby in there?"

"Pretty sure."

"It would be nice to have a little sister. Maybe even a little brother. He doesn't have to be green."

"You never know what might happen," she said as lightly as possible. "Now tell me about baking bread with Miss Rissta."

Tavi launched into a long and somewhat convoluted story about her baking prowess, but they had moved on to other things before Suzanna finally emerged from the bathroom. Joanna couldn't help a pang of envy. She had forgotten that the girl was so pretty. Her hair was long and dark, much more dramatic than Joanna's ordinary brown, and she had startling blue eyes, accentuated by the navy fabric of her borrowed outfit. The outfit was too large, but the girl had tied some artful knots in the loose fabric so that it conformed to her slender figure.

"You look very nice," she said, doing her best to sound sincere.

"It's nice to be clean." Adam made a little snuffling noise and Suzanna immediately focused on him "He's going to be hungry soon."

"Are you still feeding him?"

The girl gave a bitter laugh. "Not any more. Rulmat didn't want me that involved. But I was so desperate to get him away from there, I didn't think about what he was going to eat."

"We should go see Rissta. She's the cook, and I'm sure she can think of something."

"Leave the cabin?"

"You will have to if you want food—for Adam and for yourself," she explained as patiently as possible.

"Miss Rissta is a great cook," Tavi told her. "She's teaching Mama."

"You're working as a cook?" Suzanna looked appalled.

"There aren't exactly a lot of jobs for college professors out here," she snapped, then shook her head. "I'm sorry. It's just rather a sensitive subject."

"Umm, okay. I guess it's better than—" Fortunately, Suzanna didn't continue. Instead, she reached down and picked up Adam, whose snuffles had turned into grunts. "We should probably go before he gets really upset. He can be very loud."

CHAPTER FIFTEEN

Joanna did her best to gather her patience as they headed for the galley. She suspected the girl had been through hell, but some of her remarks had still grated on her. And then they walked into the galley and Craxan's eyes went straight to Suzanna.

"We came to see if Rissta had any suggestions on what to feed the baby," she said as pleasantly as possible, even though her nails were digging into her palms.

Suzanna was giving Craxan a worshipful smile, but then she noticed Jed and took a quick step back. "Oh, hell no. I'm not going to be in the same room with him."

"He was here first," Craxan said firmly, finally taking his eyes off of Suzanna and coming to Joanna's side, his tail wrapping around her waist.

Still annoyed, she tried to step away from him, but he only tugged her back.

"I will leave," Jed said quickly, but Joanna could see the hurt on his face. "I do not want Suzanna to be uncomfortable."

Craxan frowned at him, but he didn't make any further protest as the other male slipped away.

Rissta had been watching them all through her sharp little eyes, and now she cackled.

"I expect I have something that will work for the child. Don't the rest of you have something to do?"

"You don't need me this morning?" Joanna asked.

"Come back later."

"I want to see if Yengik has my robobeast ready," Tavi said eagerly.

Joanna looked over at Suzanna, but the girl only shrugged so she decided she wasn't needed. As she turned for the door, she almost ran into Craxan, who was back to staring at Suzanna as he edged towards the door.

What the hell was wrong with him?

She marched out of the room, and he followed her out. Tavi was already skipping ahead to find Yengik, but he put his hand on her arm to keep her at his side. She shrugged it off.

"Are you angry with me?" he asked.

"Angry? Why should I be angry? Just because you can't keep your eyes off another woman."

He looked so shocked she actually felt a little better.

"You are the only female for me, my mate."

"Then why were you staring at Suzanna?"

"You gave her the clothing I made for you."

She sighed. "I know. I wasn't thrilled about it either, but she needed something to wear. I know you put a lot of work into the clothes."

"It is not just that." His face twisted with distaste. "But her scent mingles with mine and it... distresses me."

She remembered his urgency to wash away the girl's scent earlier, and his behavior made more sense. "I'm sorry. I should have thought of that." She patted his tail. "I would suggest another shower, but I suspect I need to rescue Yengik from our daughter."

"And I need to find Jed. He will not be happy."

"He likes Suzanna, doesn't he?"

"I am afraid so. And I do not think that I can give him hope that his affections will be returned."

"I think you're right, especially after what she's been through. But we have a saying, time heals all wounds."

Sadness washed over his face. "I do not think I agree with that. Some wounds never heal."

"But maybe, with time, they ache less." She patted his tail. "Now go find your friend and I'll catch up with Tavi."

She found their daughter sitting on the floor of the small utility room where Yengik spent much of his time. The shelves were cluttered with odds and ends, but his work bench was meticulously neat and he seemed more at ease in this room than anywhere else on the ship. He gave her a shy smile as Tavi jumped up to show off her present.

The robobeast was a child's toy, somewhat like a toy she remembered from her own childhood, that could be rearranged into multiple forms. Each of the forms resembled a type of animal, and had a different pattern of movement. Tavi was delighted and immediately started to investigate all of the options.

"That's really amazing," Joanna told Yengik.

His skin turned a rather sickly shade of yellow and it took her a moment to realize he was blushing.

"I like working with my hands," he mumbled.

"Is there a lot of that here on the ship?"

He ducked his head. "Not as much as I'd hoped. The mechanics do some, but even then it's mainly routine maintenance."

"Then why are you here?"

"It was a way off of my planet," he admitted. "I know the Red Death hit us hard, but it's like everything there was going backwards. Many of my people are afraid of technology now, even though it wasn't a factor. So when the chance came to leave, I took it. I like traveling around, but..."

"Now that you know you don't like this type of work, why don't you do something else?"

He gave her a gloomy look. "Can't. I signed a seven-year contract in exchange for my passage."

"Seven years?" She stared at him in horror. "Does he even pay you?"

"A little. The captain said I didn't need many funds while I was working for him, so he is banking my credits. For when my contract is up."

That bastard. She looked over at Tavi, still playing happily. "Can you watch her for a minute? I'll be right back."

"Of course."

As soon as she left, she went looking for the captain. She found him in his office, a surprisingly plain space with everything neatly organized.

"What a pleasant surprise," he drawled. "Does your mate know you're here?"

"No." She suppressed a sudden pang of guilt. She should have told Craxan first, but she had been too angry. She suspected he wasn't going to be happy.

"And yet, somehow I don't believe that you are here to tell me that you have abandoned him for my charming self."

"Of course not. I'm here to talk to you about Yengik."

"He seems an even more unlikely choice for your affections."

"Don't be ridiculous. I'm here because you're treating him abominably. You have no right to take advantage of him like this!"

"He hasn't complained," he drawled.

"That's not the point and you know it." She glared at him. "I'm going to do everything I can to convince him not to put up with it any longer."

His lips twisted. "Good."

"What do you mean good?"

"I knew he wasn't cut out for ship life the day after he came on board. Most of them aren't."

"Most?" He wasn't making any sense.

"Most of my laborers." He picked up an old-fashioned pen and flipped it back and forth in his hands. "But they sign up anyway, and I take them away from whatever devastation they are trying to escape. Eventually they realize they have other choices and they leave. Yengik has lasted longer than most, despite my efforts to... encourage him to leave."

"Because he thinks he has an obligation to you!" she protested, but she had lost some of her vehemence.

"He has somewhat more of a conscience than usual," Merios agreed. "Even my poor behavior has not yet driven him away."

"And you've done this before? Hired a laborer and then run them off?"

He nodded, still casually flipping his pen.

"But why?"

"My planet, Kissa, was hit hard by the Red Death." For a second, he looked up at her, and the depth of pain in his eyes made her heart ache. "Do you know what it's like when most of your world has died? I was lucky. My grandfather was a merchant and we owned this ship, so I had a way to escape. Now when I can, I offer the same thing." His seriousness disappeared, replaced by his usual mocking expression. "And of course, I get some free labor out of it."

Or does he, she wondered, remembering Yengik's belief that his wages were being held for him.

"First you're saving slaves, and now you're rescuing lost boys?" she asked, still somewhat skeptical.

He smirked at her. "Don't tell anyone. It would ruin my reputation."

"I won't, but maybe you could just try talking to Yengik."

"Perhaps."

She sighed and went back to get her daughter, then returned to the kitchen. Suzanna was feeding Adam from an odd-shaped bottle, but he was sucking enthusiastically.

"I knew you'd have the answer," Joanna told Rissta, bending down to kiss her cheek. The old female actually looked shocked before she harrumphed and turned back to her pots.

The rest of the day could not have been said to be peaceful. Suzanna alternated between angry and tearful, and even though Joanna knew that they were natural reactions, she had a hard time remaining patient.

Jed came to the kitchen twice, once to offer Suzanna some cloths that could be used as diapers, and once to offer her a robe. Both times she flinched and demanded he leave, but she begrudgingly took his presents and Jed seemed satisfied with that.

As they finished up dinner preparations, Rissta shot her one of her sharp looks, then handed her a hamper filled with sealed containers.

"What's this?"

"The end of shift meal. Take it, then go find your mate, and the three of you eat together. Alone."

The idea sounded absolutely wonderful, but she hesitated, looking over at Suzanna.

"She's safe enough with me." Rissta sniffed, then gave her a push towards the door. "Now go."

Joanna took Tavi's hand and obeyed.

They found Craxan in the exercise room. He had been avoiding the kitchen, clearly uncomfortable with Suzanna's presence, and on the whole she was glad he had stayed away. But she had missed him, and watching him move through a series of controlled positions, his big body covered only by the briefest of shorts, sent a surge of excitement through her veins.

Tavi was also enthralled, although for a completely different reason. "I want to do that, Papa. Show me how."

"I will, princess, but not tonight." His gaze was hot on Joanna's face.

She held up the bag. "We have dinner. I thought maybe we could eat in our new cabin."

"That sounds like an excellent idea," he agreed, and she watched regretfully as he toweled off and pulled on the rest of his clothing.

But then he came over and kissed her while Tavi giggled, before lifting their daughter onto his shoulder.

"Let's go home," he said, and the stress of the day seemed to vanish.

The new cabin was still far from luxurious, but the main room was definitely bigger. A much larger bench could be converted into a bed for them, and, even more importantly, it had a small separate bedroom for Tavi.

"Yay, my own room!" Tavi cried. She didn't seem bothered by the fact that it was barely larger than the bunk bed, even though her room on Alliko had been so much grander.

"Your very own," Craxan said gravely, then bent down to whisper in Joanna's ear. "Which means we can do whatever we want once she's asleep."

"Good. Because there are a couple of variations on third base that I had to skip over since you wouldn't remove your pants." She brushed her hand casually against his erection as she moved away to join Tavi in admiring her room.

They ate dinner together in the main room, then Tavi played happily with her robobeast until she began to yawn. After she washed her face and brushed her teeth, Craxan carried her to bed, then stayed with them as Joanna told her stories.

She was supremely conscious of his big warm body next to hers as she talked—and of his tail stroking her hip. By the time Tavi fell asleep, her skin felt electric with excitement.

Craxan followed her back into the main cabin and flipped down the bench. He reached for her top, but she danced back out of reach.

"You first."

He obeyed willingly, his clothes flying as he stripped. His massive cock stood straight up, and she trailed her fingers lightly over the nubbed surface, her nipples beading against her shirt.

"Sit down," she whispered, and once again he obeyed.

It wasn't until she knelt in front of him that he seemed to realize what she had in mind. His eyes blazed, but he put his hand on her shoulder.

"Wait."

"Why? Do you still think it's forbidden?"

He shuddered, and she watched in fascination as a drop pearled on the tip of his cock. When she leaned forward to lick it off, he made no attempt to prevent her.

Mmm, he tasted as good as he smelled. She went back for more, swirling her tongue around the broad tip. His hands clenched so tightly on the edge of the bench that she heard the metal creak, and smiled. She continued to play, licking his tip like a lollipop, then lapping up and down his thick shaft.

"Remove your clothing," he ordered, his voice hoarse. "Please."

"Since you asked so nicely."

She sat back on her heels, then started lifting her top, gradually revealing each inch of skin. He gripped his cock, staring at her hungrily as she finally revealed her breasts, her nipples so hard they ached. She slipped out of her pants much quicker, eager to get back to him. He was so big that she wasn't sure she could get her mouth around him, but she was determined to try.

He groaned as she worked him into her mouth, and she hummed in response. Her jaw ached, but she managed to take him deeper, and deeper still until he touched the back of her throat, and then she sucked. He cried out, his fist clenching in her hair, and she pulled back.

"Do you need to put my hand over your mouth?" she teased.

"I will be quiet," he promised.

And he was, even though his body shook, and metal creaked, and she could feel his cock growing stiffer in her mouth as she worked him. Her own excitement flared to match his, and she found herself rubbing her breasts against him as his tail delved between her legs.

"You can't knot in my mouth," she gasped, and he gave a strangled assent.

His hand fisted the base of his cock, and she took him deeper, trying to reach that tight grasp. Just as her lips touched his hand, he gave a muffled groan and flooded her mouth with hot, delicious liquid. She gulped greedily, trying to swallow everything as he shuddered against her and his knot expanded to fill his hand.

"I can't believe that fits inside me," she murmured as she

reluctantly withdrew. Her own body still hovered on the edge and she couldn't wait for him to subside so he could enter her.

"We are a perfect fit," he assured her, his voice hoarse, and swung her up next to him on the bed.

"Don't we have to wait a little while?"

"Yes, but I have plans on how to fill that time."

And then his mouth was between her legs and time didn't matter.

CHAPTER SIXTEEN

Craxan slipped out of their cabin before Joanna woke. He hated to leave her, but he was worried about Jed. The other male's mood had veered wildly from hope to despair the previous day. To his relief, he found his friend in the exercise room, his face serene.

"Your calm seems enhanced this morning."

"It is. I spent most of the night wrestling with my demons, but I eventually decided I would have to take it one day at a time. Yesterday, she accepted two gifts from me."

With a great deal of reluctance, Craxan thought, but he didn't voice his opinion.

"Today I will find more ways to make her life easier."

"It would help if you could sew," he said dryly. He still hated the idea that the female was wearing his mate's clothes and mingling her scent with his.

"Of course I can sew," Jed said, frowning at him. "Why?"

"Because she will need clothing. For herself and the child."

"I gave her a robe yesterday."

"Unlike us, females seem to prefer a variety of outfits."

Jed grinned, his fangs flashing. "Excellent. I'll go at once to find out what she would like."

"If she is anything like my mate, she would like some additional sleep. Children are demanding, especially when they are young."

"I would help her with the child as well, but I don't think she'd let me."

Craxan was quite sure he was correct, but he simply changed the subject. "Then we will train and allow our females to sleep."

Jed nodded and they began. Craxan was gratified to see that Jed had already learned to apply some of the moves he had taught him. Perhaps a job as an instructor would not be so bad after all.

When he returned to their cabin, both of his females were awake. Joanna looked sleepy and satisfied, but Tavi pouted at him.

"You left me."

"I thought you were asleep."

"Well, I wasn't. Maybe I should sleep in here so you won't leave me," she suggested, giving him a hopeful look.

He darted a glance at his mate, but her shoulders were shaking with silent laughter.

"I thought you liked having your own room."

"I guess."

"Then I promise I will check every morning before I leave to see if you are awake."

"You will?"

"Yes."

She grinned and threw herself at him.

The rest of the day passed in much the same way as the previous one. He spent less time with his mate than he would have liked, because Suzanna had joined them in the kitchen again, still wearing the clothes he had given Joanna, and he hated that his scent underlaid hers. He also did not like the way she smiled at him, wishing she would smile at Jed instead. At least she had begrudgingly picked some fabric from the selection Jed had presented to her.

They ate their last meal in the cabin again at Rissta's suggestion, and for a few hours everything was right with his world. He showed Tavi a few simple moves, and discovered she had already had some defensive training. They snuggled together while Joanna told her a bedtime story. Then his mate was in his arms and nothing existed except the bliss they found in each other's embrace.

He was just reaching for her a second time when Tavi screamed. He raced into her room, Joanna right behind him.

"What is it? What's wrong?" he asked frantically, searching for intruders.

Her face was pale and damp with tears. "He left me. Father left me."

He sank down on the bed and lifted her into his arms, his heart pounding as he stroked her back with his tail.

"You know he didn't want to leave you, Tavi," Joanna said gently, smoothing the damp hair back from their daughter's face.

"I know, but he did." Her little face crumpled, but she didn't start crying again.

Joanna hummed softly as they comforted their daughter, and finally her body sagged sleepily. But when he went to put her down, her eyes flew open.

"No! Papa, don't leave me."

He looked at Joanna, and she smiled a little ruefully. "He's not going to leave you, sweetheart. Do you want to sleep with us tonight?"

"Yes, please."

"Come on then."

The three of them settled down in the big bed, and Tavi was asleep within minutes, her small body curled between them. His plans for his mate had ended sooner than he had anticipated, but he was filled with contentment as he too drifted off to sleep.

At breakfast the next morning, Jed shyly offered Suzanna and Adam two new outfits. She gave him a suspicious look, but accepted them with a muttered thanks. Relief swept over Craxan when she reappeared in the new clothing a little later. She no longer carried any trace of his scent. He felt relief and a little envy—his friend's tailoring skills were much better than his own. He would have to ask Jed for some tips.

Suzanna left again, and he remained in the kitchen with his family, entertaining Tavi and admiring the ease with which his mate moved around the kitchen. She even dared to challenge Rissta, and they had a spirited argument over the correct amount of seasoning for a grain dish. The argument was just coming to a close when he heard a scream.

"Stay here," he ordered.

He followed the sounds of a struggle into the cargo hold and found Jed pinning Anaeus face-down on the floor, one arm wrenched up behind his back. Suzanna was cowering against the wall, her new dress ripped open across her breasts.

"What happened?" Merios demanded, following him into the room.

"He... he attacked me," Suzanna sobbed. Her face was so pale she matched the color of the wall.

"I did nothing of the kind," Anaeus snarled. "The little bitch was asking—*arrgh!*"

His words ended with a scream as Craxan heard his arm snap. Jed's face was a livid mask of anger.

"Shut up," Jed ordered.

"I just wanted to see the other fabrics," Suzanna said, giving him an imploring look.

She was still sobbing, and he was afraid that she was going to throw herself at him, but then his mate joined them and drew the girl into her arms.

The captain's face was almost as angry as Jed's. "Seems you didn't get the message. Such behavior is not allowed on my ship. Throw him in the brig, Jed."

"You don't have a brig," Anaeus sneered, defiant despite his obvious pain.

Merios didn't bother to respond. He went to the far side of the hold and lifted the metal grate off of one of the storage compartments in the floor.

"In here," he ordered, and Jed obeyed.

The grate settled back in place with a loud clang, and Anaeus started to scream obscenities as Merios locked it in place.

No one gave him a second glance as they headed for the exit, but as they passed through the door, Suzanna bit her lip and turned to Jed.

"Thank you," she said softly, even though she couldn't quite look him in the eye.

"It was my honor. I am only sorry that I was not in time to prevent him from touching you."

Suzanna tugged nervously at her torn gown, but she dipped her head in acknowledgement of his words.

"Come along," Rissta said as she appeared at the end of the corridor. "Time for a meal—which we are all going to eat together." She gave them a fierce glare. "And no argument."

No one argued, and they all gathered around the big table as Rissta carved a roast beast and piled their plates high.

It was a silent meal, but not uncomfortable. No one discussed the incident with the cargo master. Suzanna no longer carried his scent which helped him relax. She also did not demand that Jed leave the room, although she chose to sit at the opposite end of the table.

As the meal came to an end, Joanna leaned against his side, while Tavi curled up in his lap.

"We will reach Rafalo's station tomorrow," Merios announced as he pushed away his empty plate. "I will warn you in advance that although it may not look... desirable, it has some hidden benefits."

Rissta shook her head. "You're always so cryptic, boy. Just spit it out."

"Since I'm sure Anaeus can't hear us, I suppose it's okay," Merios said reluctantly. "Essentially my cousin runs a rescue operation for escaped slaves. There is a secret area within the station itself, but also..."

"Oh, for pity's sake," Rissta snapped. "What he's trying *not* to tell you is that there's a colony on the surface of Tyssia which includes some humans."

Craxan frowned at her. "I thought the planet was uninhabitable."

"The upper atmosphere is poisonous, but the surface is fine," Merios said, glaring at his grandmother. "Which I was about to tell you."

"More humans?" Suzanna whispered. "Were they all taken? Like we were?"

Merios nodded uncomfortably.

"And none of us can go home?"

"It's possible that the Patrol could wipe your memory and take you back, but—" Rissta looked at the baby in Suzanna's arms, her eyes sad. "But you could not take the child."

He could almost see the temptation on the young female's face, but she looked down at her son and her arms tightened. "Then I guess I'm staying too."

The next morning, Joanna followed Craxan and Tavi onto the bridge. She wasn't sure what a spaceship bridge would be like, but it looked exactly like she would have pictured. Two chairs for Merios and Hagrin faced a complicated array of controls, while a large screen above showed the surrounding space in astonishing detail. A large circular object floated in the center of the screen, and as they grew closer, she could see the surface was pockmarked with scars and pieces of it appeared to be coming loose.

"Are you sure it's safe?" she asked doubtfully.

Merios laughed. "I warned you. But avoiding the appearance of prosperity makes it easier to avoid unwanted visitors."

"If you say so."

Craxan's tail tugged her closer. "I have been here before on business. Rafalo is a competent administrator."

A voice came over the speaker asking their business, and a few minutes later they were gliding into a large open hangar. Their final approach had revealed the size of the station and the knowledge that it was just floating there in space was surprisingly nerve-wracking.

The outer doors closed behind them, and Merios turned off the engines.

"Are you ready to meet my notorious cousin?"

"Notorious?" she whispered to Craxan as they followed him off of the bridge.

"He has a reputation as a pirate."

"Oh." *A pirate?* "Tavi, why don't you go and visit Yengik?"

"I want to see the station."

"And you can, but we're just going to talk business at first."

"Oh, all right."

Tavi skipped off, and she looked up to find Craxan smiling at her. "What?"

"You do not need to worry. He is not a bad male."

"Let me decide that," she muttered.

Her first impression was not favorable. Rafalo was an older Kissat male, flamboyantly dressed, and with the same air of mockery that Merios liked to adopt.

"Ah, Merios. Did you bring me some new victims?" he asked lazily.

Joanna tensed, but Merios just laughed.

Rafalo was accompanied by an absolutely stunning black woman with a tall, slender figure and close-cropped grey hair. She was so elegant that Joanna immediately felt small and untidy, but the woman gave her a warm smile as she elbowed Rafalo.

"I'm Alicia. Just ignore my mate. I do."

Joanna couldn't help smiling, especially when Rafalo assumed an outraged look. "I am many things, but I am not to be ignored."

Alicia did just that, speaking to Joanna as if he hadn't said anything. "I'm very pleased to meet you, although I know this is an… unfortunate situation."

She spoke as casually as if being kidnapped by aliens was of no more consequence than a parking ticket, and Joanna choked back a laugh.

"I'm Joanna. I'm happy to meet you as well."

"My mate tells me you are considering settling here. I would be delighted to show you around, both here and on the surface. Do you have a preference yet?"

"It would be easier for me to find work in the station," Craxan admitted, "although we would prefer the surface for our daughter."

Alicia's eyes lit up. "You have a child?"

"I think you're about to meet her," Joanna said, just before Tavi came flying into the room. Her robobeast was hot on her heels, making adorable little growling noises. Yengik also followed her, giving them an apologetic look.

Tavi came to a halt, her eyes widening as she took in Rafalo and Alicia, then she gave them her sunny smile. "Hello. I'm Sultavi."

"I'm very pleased to meet you, Sultavi," Alicia said, as politely as she had greeted the others. "That's a very pretty dress."

Tavi beamed. "My papa made it. And my white one is even prettier, but it's only for special occasions."

"I hope we will have a special occasion while you are here so you can wear it."

"I do too. With sweets," she added pointedly.

Joanna shook her head. They'd had a rather lengthy discussion this morning when Tavi wanted sweets for breakfast and Joanna had refused. It hadn't helped that Craxan would obviously have succumbed to their daughter's big eyes and pleading face, even though he supported her in front of Tavi.

"You can't spoil her," she'd told him after Tavi reluctantly ate a healthy breakfast and went off to find Yengik.

"I want her to be happy."

"I do too, but getting her own way all the time will not make her happy." She hesitated. "Lord K'herr did that sometimes—giving her presents instead of his time. She had just started using that to manipulate him when I came. We had a few battles at the beginning. Fortunately, she has a sweet nature and K'herr did not prevent me from disciplining her, even though I was a slave. For all his faults, I do believe he wanted the best for her."

A shadow crossed his face. "I cannot offer her many presents."

"You have love," she said firmly. "Just give her that and your time. Everything else will work out."

She remembered that conversation now as Craxan drew Rafalo aside to ask him about job prospects. His ability to provide for them obviously weighed heavily on his mind. She would ask Alicia about any cooking opportunities, she decided, but she would wait until they were alone.

The rest of the crew trickled in, even Suzanna and the baby. Alicia cooed delightedly over Adam.

"I love children," she told Joanna as she rocked the little boy. "My daughter has two, with a third on the way."

Joanna couldn't help giving her a horrified look. "Your daughter was taken too?"

Alicia laughed. "Not exactly. Daughter by love, not by birth."

"Like me," Tavi said, appearing at their side.

"That's exactly right, sweetheart."

Rissta entered with a tray full of delicacies, and Tavi danced off again.

"She's very sweet." Alicia hesitated. "Would you mind if I took her shopping? Children and clothes are my passions. And we women have to stick together out here."

Her first impulse was to say no, but she didn't see any trace of condescension in the other woman's eyes, just an unmistakable warmth.

"You're sure it's safe?" She couldn't help the nervous question. It would be the first time they had been separated since they had escaped the compound.

"Absolutely," Alicia assured her. "We'll go to the hidden part of the station and Rafalo will accompany us."

"Then I guess it's all right. If you really want to—and if you don't let her talk you into buying out the store."

"I won't." Alicia looked pleased, turning to watch as Tavi

ran over to Craxan and he lifted her into his arms. She hesitated again. "If you don't mind my asking, are you happy with your mate?"

Joanna could feel herself blushing. "Very."

"Good. My daughter is also mated to a Cire and very happy. Although that tail..." Alicia shook her head, and Joanna knew her cheeks were getting redder.

"Speaking of mates, we should rejoin ours," she said, changing the subject.

Alicia laughed, and they went to join the rest of the party.

CHAPTER SEVENTEEN

Later that day, Joanna paced back and forth at the top of the ramp. As promised, Alicia had taken Tavi shopping, with Rafalo as their guard. Joanna had been tempted to accompany them, but she had wanted a chance to talk to Craxan about their different options. Unfortunately, Merios had dragged him off for some no doubt nefarious purpose, and they hadn't returned yet. The rest of the crew had hauled Anaeus to the station authorities, then disbursed to seek entertainment. Even Suzanna and the baby were sleeping, while Jed lurked in the hall outside their door.

"So the male was right, after all. The Cire has a human female too."

The sound of the deep, mocking voice made her whirl around. A Skaal stood at the base of the ramp, and she knew immediately that he must be Adam's father. No wonder Suzanna had been so scared of Jed at first. Even though the newcomer was covered with elaborate piercings and wearing an embroidered robe, he oozed menace.

"My first thought, of course, was that one of the rival families had come after my son, but I could find no evidence," he continued, his voice casual, his eyes anything but. "Then one of my guards, a remarkably stupid male, finally thought to mention that he thought he had seen a Cire warrior later that night. It seemed a little too... coincidental."

"This is private property. You need to leave." Thankfully, her voice didn't shake.

"Property? The only property I see is you." His gaze roamed over her, and she saw the flicker of a forked tongue between his lips. "I will admit that the Cire has taste. You are far more interesting than that skinny bitch. I shall enjoy making you scream."

She couldn't suppress a shudder, and he laughed. "But that will have to wait. Where is my son?"

"I don't know what you're talking about."

"Don't play innocent with me. I know he is on board."

"And why would you think that?" she asked, playing for time. Could she find a way to alert Jed and have him get Suzanna and Adam off the ship? "Just because my mate is a Cire warrior?"

"Because that Persat idiot contacted me and confirmed it. He actually tried to sell me the information. As if I would pay the likes of him."

Anaeus had contacted him? *That bastard.* He must have done so almost as soon as they left Driguera, since Rulmat had arrived so soon after they had.

"Now give me my child," Rulmat ordered, losing the mockery.

"He's not yours, he's Suzanna's," she said defiantly.

He stared at her, then started to laugh. "You stupid female. He is *my* son. My legacy. He will inherit everything I have built —my wealth and my power. I intend to see that he is raised appropriately, surrounded by only the finest of everything.

What would his life be like with her? A useless female who only has one thing to offer—her body."

"Suzanna is not a whore," she hissed, and he laughed again.

"Perhaps not. She was a frigid little thing." He ran his eyes over her again, and she did her best not to react, even though his gaze felt like it left a trail of slime behind. "I suspect you will be a lot more enjoyable."

"You'll never get a chance to find out."

"Oh really? Who's going to stop me?"

"I am." Jed stepped up next to her, gently urging her behind him.

Rulmat gave him a contemptuous look. "Who the hell are you?"

"Jed'Ta Sa'Konin."

"The drunk responsible for the wreck of the *Farseer*?"

Jed's shoulders stiffened, but he answered calmly. "Yes."

"This would almost be amusing were it not so pathetic. Out of my way." When Jed didn't move, Rulmat sighed. "Fine. Let's get this over with."

Joanna wasn't sure what she had expected. Guns perhaps, like an old-fashioned shootout, or even swords, but instead the two males simply flew at each other, fangs and claws flashing. They met with a brutal thud, each straining to knock the other to the ground.

From what she could tell, Rulmat was older, but he had the weight advantage. He managed to force Jed down, but Jed twisted as he went, locking his legs around Rulmat and carrying him down as well. Then Rulmat roared and a splatter of blue blood hit the floor. Jed clutched his arm, and Joanna started to panic.

She looked around desperately for some kind of weapon, but the heavy crates filling the hold were sealed tight. More blood slicked the floor, but Rulmat's scales glistened and she thought Jed had managed to use his claws on the other male.

"No! No, he can't be here!" The shocked cry came from the interior of the hold, and she looked up to see Suzanna standing there, her face white and her hands pressed to her mouth.

"Go back to the cabin," Joanna ordered. "Get inside and lock the door."

If Rulmat defeated Jed, he would still have to find Suzanna, and she could only pray that Craxan would have returned before he did.

But it was too late. Suzanna didn't move, her body frozen in place, and Rulmat looked up and saw her. He grinned, his fangs stained with blue blood.

"You didn't think I was going to let him go, did you?"

A spark of defiance replaced the horrified shock. "You'll never take him away from me."

"Stupid—" Rulmat's words were cut off as Jed roared and attacked again.

She had thought the battle brutal before, but this was even more intense. Their bodies slammed against each other, blood spraying. Jed fought like a male possessed, and gradually seemed to gain the upper hand. Rulmat's responses slowed, barely evading Jed's blows. Then Jed caught Rulmat around the neck, tightening his grip as Rulmat thrashed and choked and finally went limp.

"Is he dead?" Suzanna whispered as Jed released Rulmat.

"I don't think so," Joanna said. "His chest is still moving."

Jed bent down over the other male, hissing at him.

"She is not your female. He is not your son. Leave now and never return."

As he started to stand, Joanna saw the flash of metal.

"Jed, watch out!"

He turned and grabbed Rulmat's wrist. They wrestled for

control of the knife, and she watched in horror as Rulmat poised it over Jed's throat. Jed seemed to sag in defeat, but then he twisted beneath Rulmat, lightning fast, and the knife plunged into Rulmat's chest instead. An almost shocked expression crossed the arrogant male's face and his mouth opened, blue blood trickling from his lips, but only a garbled sound emerged before his body jerked and went still.

"Now he's dead," Joanna said, her voice shaking.

"Good." Suzanna's voice seemed unnaturally calm.

She walked steadily over to the body and looked down at it, her face expressionless. Then she drew back her foot and kicked the body, over and over, while tears streamed down her face. Jed started to reach for her, but looked down at his bloody hands and hesitated, giving Joanna a helpless look.

She went to the girl, making the same soothing noises she would have used with Tavi, and gently put her hand on Suzanna's arm. Suzanna jerked away from her, but she finally stopped kicking the body.

As Joanna tried to decide what to do next, the hangar doors slammed open and Craxan and Merios raced in, followed by some unknown males. Relief swept over her at the sight of him, but then she saw the blood dripping down his arm as he reached her.

"You're hurt!" she cried, as he wrapped his arms and tail around her with a sigh of relief.

"Thank Granthar. You are not injured?"

"No, I'm fine. Jed stopped Rulmat from laying a hand on either of us. But what happened to you?"

"Rulmat's guards," he said grimly. "They surrounded the hangar, but the station monitor caught sight of them and warned Merios. We returned as quickly as we could." His arms tightened. "I was terrified that we would not make it in time."

"But you did," she said soothingly. "Although I don't understand. If he had guards with him, why did he come alone? Why didn't he just use them to take over the ship?"

"Because he is—*was*—an arrogant bastard. I suspect he wanted to prove that he did not need any help to retrieve his child. He did not count on Jed."

They both looked over at where Jed was huddled on a step, his face haunted.

"This will be hard on him," Craxan said softly. "He swore never to be responsible for the loss of another life."

"He didn't have a choice."

"I believe you. I just hope he will believe it."

As they watched, Suzanna approached Jed. She was still pale, her face tear-stained, but she walked all the way to Jed's side. For the briefest second, her hand touched his shoulder. He looked up at her, and their eyes met. Then she turned and fled, but his eyes followed her out of the room, and then he smiled.

"I think he will," she said, and leaned against Craxan's side. "When is Tavi coming back?"

"Not for a while. Merios sent word to Rafalo, and he will keep Alicia and Tavi away from here until we can... clean up."

"Do you have to help?"

"I intended to volunteer. Why?"

"Because I need you." She reached for his tail, clutching it in her hand. "I... I thought I was going to end up as a slave again. That I would never see you and Tavi again."

"If he had taken you, I would not have stopped until I found you again. There is no place in this universe where he could have hidden you from me." He growled and swept her up in his arms, carrying her quickly through the corridors. "You are mine, Joanna."

"You know, I've been thinking," Joanna said to him, a long time later.

She was curled against his side, her fingers idly stroking his chest, the action both soothing and arousing.

"What have you been thinking?"

"I was thinking of what Rulmat said. Of wanting a son to carry on his legacy."

His mouth twisted with distaste. "And he would stop at nothing to achieve his goal."

"He was an evil male," she agreed. "But it made me think. I don't believe that Lord K'herr was evil."

"I disagree. He bought you as a slave."

She sighed. "I know, and I'm not trying to make excuses for him. But he didn't treat me badly, or allow anyone else to do so. He was just focused on Sultavi. That's why he worked so hard—to create a legacy for her."

"I am not sure I understand." Although he was afraid he did.

"We—I—took her away from her home."

"In order to keep her safe."

"I know. And at the time, I didn't have another choice. But now I'm wondering if maybe we should try and restore the legacy her father wanted to give her. It just seems wrong to let Lord T'paja get away with stealing it from her."

"I am not sure it would be possible," he said slowly.

"Doesn't Alliko have a system of law? I overheard his guards saying he wanted Sultavi in order to legitimize his claim. That implies it could be questioned."

"Are you sure about this? If we stay here, you would have the company of other humans."

"I admit it would be nice, and from what Alicia told me, the planet is beautiful." She lifted up on her elbow and studied him, her face pleading. "I'm sure we could be happy here, but I want to do what's best for Tavi."

He sighed heavily. "Perhaps you are right."

"Is it possible, do you think? To reclaim her home?"

"I am not sure. But perhaps I could make some inquiries."

"Thank you, Craxan. I just want our daughter to have everything to which she is entitled."

"I know, Joanna." He rolled over on top of her, loving the way her body cradled him. "Now are you through with your thinking?"

"Maybe. Why?" Her eyes sparkled up at him.

"Because I suspect that we will not remain uninterrupted for much longer, and I have an idea about base four point six."

"You do have some very creative bases," she admitted.

He proceeded to prove her correct.

"You want to do what?" Merios stared at Joanna and Craxan.

Although she had responded deliciously to his lovemaking, she had been anxious to put a plan in place so he had taken her to see the captain.

"We want to return to Alliko and reclaim Sultavi's legacy," she said calmly.

Merios raised an eyebrow. "Good luck with that. But I'm not sure why you're telling me."

"Because we would like you to take us."

"I think you're forgetting Trevelor—the planet you were once so insistent on reaching? I have cargo that is destined for there."

Considering the multiple delays he had incurred so far, Craxan doubted there was any urgency to the delivery, but Joanna nodded patiently.

"And you can still take it. After a little detour to Alliko."

Merios studied his claws. "Just how do you intend to pay for this... detour?"

His mate shot him a doubtful glance, and he nodded. They both had some hesitation over this part of her plan, but hadn't been able to come up with an alternative. "Tavi's biological father was a very wealthy male."

"She doesn't seem to have inherited his wealth," Merios said dryly.

"Because of how quickly we left. But if we return and if we can get access to her inheritance, we can pay you for the trip. A reasonable amount," she added quickly.

"It sounds like a lot of *ifs*."

She shrugged. "Maybe it's a little bit of a gamble. But don't you enjoy taking a chance? Or is that only on people?"

Merios started to laugh as Craxan gave her a puzzled look.

"You have a devious mate, Craxan. But I will agree to the journey—for a *generous* remuneration."

"I doubt we have the same definition of generous," she said. "But you will be well paid."

"Then I will have Hagrin set course for Alliko. And I hope you know what you're doing," Merios said over his shoulder as he left them.

"Do we know what we're doing?" she asked him.

No. But he was not going to add to her worries. Instead, he told her truthfully, "We are trying to do what is best for our daughter."

She sighed and squeezed his hand. "I hope so."

CHAPTER EIGHTEEN

Craxan slipped through the concealed door that Joanna remembered from when she and Tavi had escaped the Sodan compound. The lush gardens were quiet, but he could hear the sound of drunken laughter from the gatehouse and he shook his head. He paused for a few minutes to check for activity, but no one bothered to patrol the grounds.

T'paja was far too confident. Perhaps he assumed that his efforts to intimidate the occupants of Isokau had been successful. Instead, the opposite had occurred. The more he let his warriors roam unchecked, the more the townspeople had come to dislike him.

If he had simply stepped into Lord K'herr's shoes and carried on as before, there would have been some disgruntled comments but little more. Instead, they had returned to find Isokau on the brink of rebellion.

They had arrived back on Alliko the previous night, and as soon as the ship had docked, he and Joanna, heavily cloaked, had gone to visit Opinnas.

The elderly scholar greeted them with a troubled frown.

"Your presence here worries me. But I think perhaps it is necessary."

He told them what had been happening while they were gone, but Craxan had seen much of it for himself on the way to the scholar's house. Broken windows, scrawled graffiti, and a restless, violent energy. Even the guards who had formerly watched over the spaceport were no longer present.

"Do you think the Tribunal will rule in Sultavi's favor?" Joanna asked. They had spent much of the trip investigating the laws of Alliko. The Tribunal was the titular authority over the various Houses, and they had decided it was their best option.

"There are no guarantees, but Lord K'herr was popular. T'paja is not. The Houses have long memories and his family is not respected." Opinnas adjusted the spectacles resting on his beak. "But it will not be a fast process. And once he receives notice that he is being challenged, he will leave no feather unplucked in his efforts to find Sultavi."

"Maybe we should go back to Tyssia while we wait," Joanna said anxiously.

Opinnas shook his crest. "I'm afraid you will need to be here to bring the action."

It was because of that conversation that he was here now, investigating T'paja's defenses. *Which are minimal at best,* he thought disgustedly as he strolled towards the building intended for the ruler of the House.

Two guards were stationed outside the main entrance, but since they were passing a bottle back and forth, Craxan had no trouble slipping past them and around the side of the building. Joanna had sketched out a rough floor plan, so he headed for the bedroom intended for the lord of House Sodan. Light spilled out of the long windows that opened onto a paved terrace. He edged closer but could only see a portion of the interior.

"There will be trouble, Lord T'paja," a voice warned, clearly audible through the open windows.

From his hidden position, Craxan could see the speaker. An older warrior, his neat uniform a striking contrast to the slovenly guards Craxan had seen so far.

"Don't be foolish, Ottan. Who's going to challenge me? I am the ruler of House Sodan now." The second voice practically purred with satisfaction.

Ottan cleared his throat. "Officially, the title remains with the child."

Something flew past Ottan's head, but he didn't flinch, even when the object hit the wall and exploded into glittering shards.

"Because you were too incompetent to find her," T'paja snarled.

"My information suggests that she left the planet."

Craxan frowned. Did the guard actually know something, or was he just humoring the temperamental lord?

"Then she has no claim," T'paja said.

"She would only have to return and establish her identity."

"Then make sure you are watching the spaceport. Do I have to specify everything?"

"I am watching it," Ottan said calmly, and Craxan jerked.

The bush that concealed him rustled, but he was more concerned with the implications of the older male's words. Had the absence of guards at the spaceport been a decoy?

"Good. If she dares show her face, eliminate her."

Every muscle in Craxan's body clenched as rage swept over him. The bastard dared to threaten his daughter?

"I beg your pardon?" For the first time, a hint of emotion

crossed Ottan's face. "You said you wanted to bring her here so you could claim her as your ward."

"I've decided that is no longer necessary." T'paja's hand came into view, heavily laden with rings, as he gestured dismissively. "No one is challenging my rulership. It would be easier just to eliminate her."

"But she is just a child."

"Then it shouldn't be a difficult job. Now leave me. One of my males is bringing me a... visitor."

Ottan stared at him, then bowed stiffly. "Yes, Lord T'paja."

The guard didn't leave through the doorway. Instead, he headed for the long windows. Craxan drew back into the shadows, his hand resting on his knife.

Ottan stepped out onto the terrace, then strolled casually towards Craxan's hiding place. He stopped a short distance away to light a thin cigar.

"My loyalty has never been questioned before," he said softly. "But I will not be responsible for the death of a child."

The old guard moved away without another word, leaving Craxan frowning after him. Ottan obviously knew that he was there, but he had made no effort to stop him.

Tonight had only been intended to gather information, to identify T'paja's weaknesses, but after what he had just heard, that plan had changed. T'paja had threatened his daughter. Unacceptable.

Craxan's hand dropped to his knife as he headed for the open windows.

ONCE AGAIN, JOANNA FOUND HERSELF PACING ANXIOUSLY, this time outside the ship. When they landed on Alliko, Merios parked the ship in one of the ordinary slots allotted to cargo ships. It connected to a small warehouse designed for loading and unloading cargo, but since they weren't doing either, there was plenty of room for her pacing and she didn't have to worry about being seen.

"I'm just not cut out to be a mercenary's mate," she muttered to herself. Craxan had gone off to scout the compound and evaluate T'paja's defenses. In theory, it seemed much less difficult than stealing a child from a dangerous criminal, but at least she hadn't known about that one until it was over.

Suzanna had told her what Craxan must have done to get Adam, and it had made her blood run cold. She thought the girl was trying to be helpful, but it only made her more nervous to know the type of risks he was capable of taking. It was actually a relief when Suzanna went off to attend to her son.

Joanna was still shocked that the girl had decided to accompany them. She had expected her to be thrilled with the prospect of settling down on Tyssia, but she had asked to stay on board instead. Apparently, she felt safer with Craxan around. And even Jed, she had admitted. Joanna wasn't thrilled about her continued hero worship of Craxan, but at least it never went further than a few doe-eyed glances.

"Mama!" Tavi came flying down the ramp towards her, Rissta a few steps behind.

"What's the matter, sweetheart? You're supposed to be in bed."

"I was, but I woke up and no one was there." A bottom lip pouted out. "Papa said he would see if I was awake before he left."

"In the morning," she reminded her. "And this is not the morning."

"You see, Tavi?" Rissta added. "That's what I told you."

"But I don't like it!"

"You can't like every-" She and Rissta began at the same time, then they both laughed.

"Do you want me to take her back to bed?" the other female asked, but Joanna shook her head.

"No, it's all right. She can keep me company for a while."

"I'll make some shoko. That might calm her down." Those sharp blue eyes studied Joanna. "I'll make enough for both of you."

"Thank you, Rissta. For everything," she said sincerely.

Rissta sniffed, but she was obviously pleased.

"Tell me a story," Tavi demanded.

That put an end to her pacing, but she wasn't ready to return to the ship yet. There was a small office attached to the warehouse and she remembered seeing some seating in there. She had barely started the story when Tavi jumped up and moved restlessly around the room.

"What's wrong, sweetheart?"

"We're back in Isokau, right?"

"That's right."

"And Papa is going to get rid of the bad man so I can go home again?"

"That's the plan," she said as confidently as possible.

"But I don't want to go home!" The words burst out as a tear appeared on Tavi's cheek.

Joanna's heart sank. She had never considered the possibility that Tavi might not want to return. Were the memories too hard for her?

"Why not?" she asked gently.

"Because Papa will go away and you won't be my mama anymore."

Her heart ached at the pain on her daughter's face. "Tavi, I am always going to be your mama, no matter where we are."

"Really?" Tavi gave her a hopeful look. "But you weren't before."

Several explanations sprang to mind, but she settled for the simplest. "You may not have called me that, but I knew you were my daughter the moment I met you."

"Your heart daughter?"

"Exactly."

Tavi threw her arms around her neck, hugging her fiercely. She could feel the dampness of tears against her neck, and she had to hold back her own.

"I can still call you Mama, even here?" Tavi asked at last.

"Yes, sweetheart. Even here."

"And Papa isn't going to go away?"

"No. We're a family now, and families stay together."

Tavi gave a sigh of satisfaction, and her small body relaxed.

"I want some shoko now," she announced, a few minutes later.

"Do you want to go and see if Miss Rissta has finished making it?"

"Okay."

Tavi jumped up and started for the door leading into the warehouse, but as she did, the outer door opened and an Allikan male stepped inside.

It was Besu.

Joanna's heart started to pound as she saw him look from her to Tavi, and his lips curled into a twisted grin.

"Well, isn't this nice? The two of you are going to make me a very wealthy male."

He tried to grab Tavi, and she kicked him in the shins. It was one of the moves Craxan had been teaching her, and although Joanna doubted it had hurt him, it startled him enough that he let her go.

"Run, Tavi," she yelled. "Run!"

Her daughter darted out of the room, and Besu snarled as he turned back to her. "I'll find her soon enough. But I guess I'll just have to start with you."

"Don't you dare touch me," she hissed. "My mate will kill you."

"Mate?" His mouth twisted into a cruel sneer. "No one is going to mate a primitive human. You're only good for fucking."

He came a step closer, and she braced herself, ready to kick out as soon as he was within range.

"That is where you are wrong." Craxan's familiar voice was taut with anger as he stalked into the room.

Besu took one look at him, and his already ashy skin paled. "I... I didn't mean it like that."

"Yes, you did."

Craxan stalked towards him, and Besu tried to feint to one side. Craxan caught him, grabbed his neck and twisted. Joanna heard Besu's neck snap with a sickening crack before Craxan tossed his body aside and rushed over to her.

"Are you all right? Did he hurt you?"

"I'm fine," she assured him, even though tears were pouring down her cheeks. "Where's Tavi?"

"With Merios and Rissta. They are just outside but I did not want her to see this."

"What happened at the compound?"

"T'paja is dead," he said in a satisfied voice.

"I thought you were only going to scout."

He shrugged a shoulder. "I decided there was no purpose in waiting."

"Does that mean we can take her home?"

"I will have to replace the staff first, but yes. She is once again Lady Sultavi of House Sodan."

Relief washed over her. Craxan and Tavi were both safe and unharmed, and they would have a home together.

"I thought you would be happy," he said, his tail coming up to caress her damp cheek.

"I am. I just can't believe it's over."

"Only the bad parts," he assured her. "Now we have the rest of our lives to be together, to enjoy our daughter, and to love each other."

And as he bent his head to kiss her, she knew that he was right.

EPILOGUE

O*ne year later...*

CRAXAN STROLLED THROUGH THE DARK GARDENS OF THE compound. He liked doing this last check at night, liked knowing that everything was secure. A patrolling guard nodded respectfully and continued on his way, his eyes alert. The training program for the guards was coming along well, and he found a great deal of satisfaction in the job, although more and more of his time was occupied with managing the affairs of House Sodan.

The Tribunal had granted them legal guardianship of Sultavi and he was determined that her legacy would be preserved. Fortunately, he and Joanna divided the duties between them so they still had plenty of time with their family.

As he passed the kitchens, he could hear Rissta scolding an unfortunate assistant. From the tone of her voice, he could tell she liked the young male, but he doubted the male would believe that. Everyone had been shocked when Rissta announced that she was coming with them to take over the compound kitchens. He had ventured to suggest that they would be happy for her just to live with them.

She had smacked his shoulder, a surprisingly strong blow, and laughed. "You don't want that. If I'm not cooking, I get a little grouchy."

Now she ruled over the kitchens with an iron hand and seemed extremely satisfied. Merios had accepted her decision with a casual shrug, but given his frequent visits, Craxan suspected he missed the old woman. He was due to arrive tomorrow, along with the rest of the crew, including Yengik. The young male had somewhat surprisingly decided to remain on the ship, although he had worked out an agreement with Merios and was also developing a line of mechanical toys. Rafalo and Alicia were coming as well, and Tavi was eagerly anticipating a new dress from Auntie Alicia.

Pots clattered inside the kitchen, and he ducked his head through the door to find Rissta glaring at her assistant as he stacked dishes with a trembling hand.

"You are up late, Rissta."

"Mating feasts don't cook themselves," she said tartly.

"You are supposed to be a guest," he reminded her, but she only shrugged.

"So I'm both. Now let me get back to work."

He accepted the inevitable and withdrew. Suzanna had finally consented to accept Jed as her mate, and they were having a ceremony the following day. Craxan had watched in bemusement as Jed had wooed her slowly and patiently over the past year. Thank Granthar his own mating had been accomplished in far less time.

Thinking of his mate made him hurry down the path and into the family quarters. He found Joanna in their bedroom, reading in the soft light. Their son Vani was asleep at her breast. He still couldn't believe that he had both a daughter and a son. They had named him after Vanha, and the night he was born, Craxan had lifted a silent toast to his friend and mentor, sure that somewhere he was smiling.

As he drew closer to the bed, he could see Tavi curled up asleep on Joanna's other side.

"I see you have company," he said softly as he crossed to her side.

She looked up and smiled at him, beautiful in the lamplight. Her pregnancy had been difficult for her, and there would be no more children, but she was once more healthy and glowing. *Very healthy*, he thought appreciatively as his gaze traveled down over the lush breasts she had uncovered to feed their son.

"Tavi had a nightmare," she said, immediately diverting his attention.

"Is she all right?" They had occurred several times after they returned to the compound, but it had been months since the last time, and he had hoped that they had finally ceased.

"She is now. Rouvi was here today, bringing ale for the mating feast, and I think it reminded her of when we were hiding." Her face softened. "Waiting for you to come and save us."

"I think the two of you are the ones who saved me."

It was a familiar argument, and she only shook her head, her eyes warm.

"Why don't you carry her back to bed? I'll see if I can get Vani back in his crib without waking him." He followed her gaze and saw that their son was still latched onto her nipple. He seemed to be asleep, but Craxan knew from experience that he didn't like being removed from that position. He couldn't blame his son; he was very fond of his mate's nipples as well.

His tail curved around her other breast at the thought, gently circling the taut peak, and he heard her breath catch.

"Tavi, bed. Vani, crib," she whispered. "Then it's our turn."

He pressed a quick kiss to his mouth, then picked up his sleeping daughter. Once they moved in, they had rearranged the rooms and her bedroom, while still grand, was only a short distance from theirs.

As he put her into her bed, her eyes opened.

"Papa."

"Hello, princess."

"I had a bad dream."

"I know. Mama told me. Do you want to talk about it?"

She shook her head vehemently, dark purple locks flying. "No. But will you stay with me for a while?"

His mate was waiting, but his daughter needed him. He sat down next to her and she snuggled closer.

"Tell me about how you found us."

It was her favorite story, retold so many times that it bore little resemblance to the actual events, but that didn't matter. What mattered was the fundamental truth - he had found them and claimed them as his.

"It was a dark and stormy night," he began.

By the time Tavi was asleep and he returned to their bedroom, the room was dark and quiet. He undressed and slid quietly into bed. As much as he wanted to wake his mate, she needed her sleep.

"You were gone a long time," she murmured.

"Tavi wanted me to tell her our story." He drew her into the curve of his body, his tail settling over her stomach. "She never gets tired of it."

"Neither do I." She began stroking his tail, lightly scratching her blunt little nails along the sensitive length, and he shuddered.

"You know what that does to me," he warned.

"Of course. Why do you think I'm doing it?" She gave a teasing wiggle, the soft curves of her ass caressing his already rigid erection.

"You are not too tired?"

"Tired of waiting for you to take a hint. Is this better?"

She twisted around in his arms, and then the sweet warmth of her mouth closed over his cock and he lost the ability to speak. Fortunately, he did not lose the ability to move and his tail dipped between her legs, finding her already wet and ready for him. He pulled away from her mouth, despite her murmured protest, and placed his cock at her entrance. He pressed slowly against the tight opening until she gave that soft gasp he loved so much and flowered open around him.

Usually, he left a light on so that he could appreciate her lush beauty, but tonight the surrounding darkness let him concentrate on the other details of their joining. The way her breath hitched as he slid deeper into her silky cunt. The way her scent increased, making his head swim. The way her breasts pressed against his chest, the hard peaks damp with milk. The way her skin tasted as he buried his head in her neck.

They rocked together in the darkness, a long, slow slide into pleasure until she shivered and her channel fluttered wildly around him, and he could no longer resist the urgings of his body. His hips jerked forward, burying his cock deep inside as his knot expanded, locking them together.

Her legs and arms wrapped around him, holding him just as tightly, and she sighed happily.

"Have I ever told you how much I love it when we're together like this?"

"You do seem to enjoy it," he agreed. "But then you seem to enjoy all of the bases."

She laughed, and the vibration made his cock jerk.

"I do, because we're reaching them together." Her lips brushed against his cheek as they had done the first night they met, and then her breathing deepened as she drifted off to sleep.

How well he remembered that day. He had been so empty—and now he was overflowing. He had a mate, a family, friends, more happiness than he had ever dared to hope for.

He held his mate as she slept and smiled into the darkness.

AUTHORS' NOTE

Thank you so much for reading *The Nanny and the Alien Warrior!* We hope you enjoyed our sweet and steamy story! As always, found family plays a huge role in this book - as does love, in all its many guises.

Fun fact about the heroine in this story...

We chose the name Joanna because it's a mashup of our debut SFR heroines: Anna from Honey's *Anna and the Alien* and Seph (Josephine) from Bex's *Thanemonger*. Kudos to those who figured out that bit of trivia beforehand!

We want to express our undying gratitude to our beta readers, Janet S., Nancy V., and Kitty S. Thank you, ladies, for helping us perfect our story!

We also want to give a huge thank you to Cameron Kamenicky and Naomi Lucas, the amazing graphic designers who created our outstanding cover. They perfectly captured the relationship between Craxan and Tavi.

Lastly, we'd like to thank our families. The support of our spouses and children has been phenomenal. We couldn't do it without you!

AUTHORS' NOTE

Again, thank you so much for reading our book! It would mean the world if you left an honest review at Amazon. Reviews help other readers find books to enjoy, which helps the authors as well!

All the best,
Honey & Bex

The next book in the *Treasured by the Alien* series will be coming in late fall 2021!

Honey's next book, **Kate and the Kraken,** is coming at the end of July!

When rebellious Prince A'tai rescues a stolen human scientist, she may turn out to be the key not only to his happiness, but to the future of his planet!

Kate and the Kraken is available on Amazon!

For all the latest updates, teasers, and recommendations, please visit our websites!

www.honeyphillips.com
www.bexmclynn.com

OTHER TITLES

Treasured by the Alien
with Bex McLynn

Mama and the Alien Warrior

A Son for the Alien Warrior

Daughter of the Alien Warrior

A Family for the Alien Warrior

The Nanny and the Alien Warrior

Cosmic Fairy Tales

The Ugly Dukeling by Bex McLynn

Jackie and the Giant by Honey Phillips

BOOKS BY HONEY PHILLIPS

The Alien Abduction Series

Anna and the Alien

Beth and the Barbarian

Cam and the Conqueror

Deb and the Demon

Ella and the Emperor

Faith and the Fighter

Greta and the Gargoyle

Hanna and the Hitman

Izzie and the Icebeast

Joan and the Juggernaut

Kate and the Kraken

The Alien Invasion Series

Alien Selection

Alien Conquest

Alien Prisoner

Alien Breeder

Alien Alliance

Alien Hope

Exposed to the Elements

The Naked Alien

The Bare Essentials

A Nude Attitude

The Buff Beast

The Strip Down

Cyborgs on Mars

High Plains Cyborg

The Good, the Bad, and the Cyborg

A Fistful of Cyborg

A Few Cyborgs More

The Magnificent Cyborg

The Outlaw Cyborg

Anthologies

Alien Embrace

Standalone Books

Krampus and the Crone - An SFR Holiday Tale

Books by Bex McLynn

Standalone Books

Rein: A Tidefall Novel

The Ladyships Series

Sarda

Thanemonger

Bane

Manufactured by Amazon.ca
Bolton, ON

32158566R00118